Summer Fling

Tales of Seduction

A Temptation Press

Anthology

Summer Fling

Tales of Seduction

A Temptation Press Anthology

© 2017 Temptation Press – an Imprint of Zimbell House Publishing
Book and Cover Design by The Book Planners
A division of Zimbell House Publishing

Published in the United States by Temptation Press
All Rights Reserved

Trade Paper ISBN: 978-1-945967-71-9
Kindle ISBN: 978-1-945967-72-6
Digital ISBN: 978-1-945967-73-3
Library of Congress Control Number: 2017908197

First Edition: June/2017
10 9 8 7 6 5 4 3 2 1

Acknowledgements

Temptation Press would like to thank all those that contributed to this anthology. We chose to showcase nine new voices that best represented our vision for this work.

We would also like to thank our Temptation Press team for all their hard work and dedication to these projects.

Finally, a special shout-out to *The Book Planners* for creating yet another wonderful cover design.

Contents

Candy Silver's Summer Fling

E. W. Farnsworth

The Whalebone Motel on the seaside was just as Candy Silver remembered from her family' childhood visits. She had driven to Nags Head straight from Chapel Hill after her hardest semester. She wanted to forget the pressure of finishing her degree and sink back into a nostalgic past that had no links with biochemistry. Destined to enter medical school in the fall, she would begin another run through a three-year maze that would lead to her MD credential. She did not want to think about the future. As she dragged her bags from the car into her room, she thought about the luxury of spending three months with no schedule, no homework, and no overeager, immature male coeds.

It was not that she hated men. Candy was a red-blooded woman. She liked men when she could compartmentalize their attentions. What she did not need as she pursued her studies was a distraction, particularly one that might permanently upset her long-term plans. The men she had dated so far had only wanted a temporary relationship. She cut off Fred Raspberry's occasional dates when he mentioned wanting to get married right after college. Bill Stormly became fixated on sex with no thoughts about the future, so she had to discourage him too.

The last thing she needed was to repeat her mother's pattern of departing from a career as a research chemist to raise a family. She saw the raw disappointment in her mother's eyes whenever she discussed the events that led to her pregnancy. According to her mother's account, she had been taken by surprise one summer's day. Her life was changed utterly for ten minutes of rapture. There was no going back.

Her mother's sage advice returned to her mind whenever she had been tempted, "Candace, you must make your own choices in life. You'll have to accept the consequences of your choices. So choose wisely. Don't act impulsively. If you have goals, achieve them."

Fred had promised her fabulous wealth and social position— four years too soon. On the other hand, Bill had promised her ten minutes of pleasure followed by a lifetime of ruin. She was physically attracted to him, but she restrained him from doing more than hot petting, and finally, she had drawn the line. Handsome and attentive as he was, he had no enduring vision, and he certainly didn't want to consider her vision of earning a medical degree.

Candy shook her head as she unpacked her bags. She tucked her undies in the top drawer of the dresser and stopped to look in the mirror. She thought she still looked young. Her eyes looked a little strained, but she had no crows' feet. She had maintained her figure through these first crucial college years and was pleased with what she saw when she turned sideways to examine her silhouette.

Returning to her task, the dresser drawers filled up as her soul emptied. Her eyes filled with tears as she let her frustrations go and sat on the side of the bed until her cry was over. Suddenly ravenously hungry, Candy decided to drive back up the strip to the seafood restaurant for dinner.

As she was coming out of her cabin, a tall, handsome man appeared out of nowhere. He had a healthy tan, blond hair, and the bluest eyes. Candy tried to seem unaffected by the man's unabashed staring.

"Good afternoon. I'm in the next cabin over. Why don't we get acquainted over dinner?"

His offer was good natured and bold. Candy was caught between surprise and outrage. She thought, *I was on my way to dinner anyway. What will it hurt to have dinner with this dishy next-door neighbor?*

She extended her hand with a smile, "Hi, my name is Candy Silver. What's yours?"

He beamed at her and shook her hand, "Hi Candy. My name's Skip Loridge. Do you like seafood?"

"Yes, I do. It's one of the reasons I'm staying here. I know a restaurant right down the strip. They serve the best seafood in North Carolina. Shall we take your car or mine?"

He gestured toward his Jaguar. "Let's take my ride. I don't drink, so I'll be able to get us home safely. We'll be back in time for a leisurely walk on the beach if you like."

Candy and Skip climbed into his metallic blue Jag. In five minutes, they were climbing out again at the Surf Rider Restaurant and Bar. Candy could not tell whether the heads they turned were ogling him, her, or the pair of them as a couple. She knew the look of catty jealousy in the eyes of some of the women. She also thought she knew the calculations going through the minds of the beach bums who were trying to imagine how she would look without her short-shorts and halter.

Skip had the head waiter take them to a table out back with a view to the surf. Candy liked the way this man took charge. She also liked the way he moved, with confidence and power. When they had received their menus and ice water, Candy said, "I want this to be Dutch treat with no strings attached."

"Whatever the lady wishes, shall be so!" He said this as he examined the menu. "You recommended this place. What do you think we should order?"

She smiled. "I'm going to have their signature she-crab soup, a summer salad, and broiled flounder with small potatoes. Whatever you choose, save room for dessert. The key lime pie is to die for. They use real key limes, the little ones."

"It sounds good to me. I'll order the same. I also want a side dish of sliced lemon and lime for my ice water. I know I don't know you from college. You don't look like you're from Beast Campus."

"So you're from Duke. I'm from Chapel Hill. Are you a Greek?"

"I'm Theta Chi. This was my senior year. I'm here at Nags Head for two weeks. Then I'll be joining my dad and brother on wildcat oil rigs in the Arabian Sea."

"Are your people in oil and gas?"

"We've been in the oil patch for three generations. Each generation has built its fortune in oil. I'll get my feet on the ground this summer. Then I'll be off to the four corners of the world looking for a wildcat strike."

"Isn't that dangerous work?"

The waiter interrupted their conversation to take their orders. When he disappeared, Skip continued, "The work can be dangerous because oil and gas come up from underground mixed with toxic gasses that are not easily detected. Political risks are also endemic to the trade. Most of the best wells are situated where the political dynamics are spoty. But most of the work is grueling manual labor in the hot sun. Typically, I work eighteen to twenty hours a day, seven days a week. But enough about me. What are you doing here in Nags Head?" He ate his she-crab soup, but his eyes never left hers.

"I just finished pre-med studies, and I've been accepted at Hopkins for their MD program in the fall. My family has always vacationed here. I'm also spending a couple of weeks here. Then I'll head home to Roanoke and work in my parent's furniture business until it's time to drive to school in Maryland."

"Congratulations on making it through the pre-med and on getting into Hopkins. You must be a lot smarter than I am."

She reddened and looked down at her salad. "I'm pretty good at memorizing scads of facts. Also, I'm careful to exclude diversions."

"You look like you keep fit. Apparently, you haven't excluded working out, some would consider that a diversion." His eyes swept over her body appreciatively.

She was uncertain where to take their conversation after his allusion to her body. "How would it look for a future doctor to be out of shape? One of my interests is improving patient care before a disorder strikes."

"Do you mean homeopathic medicine?" He sipped his ice water then squeezed some lime into his glass and stirred it with his spoon.

"That's part of it. Exercise is another. What kind of workout do you prefer?" Candy figured turnabouts are fair play! She could see his muscles tense as her eyes scanned his body.

"I play basketball and tennis. I also lift weights twice a week. I don't do anything awfully strenuous, but I exercise constantly. It keeps my mind alert and off trouble."

She smiled at the word, 'trouble.' "And what kind of trouble are you trying to avoid?"

"Women largely. Don't get me wrong, I like women a lot. But the oil patch wreaks havoc on relationships. Dad is on his third wife. The other two divorced him. They had enough of living in Quonset huts and waiting for Dad to return from one of his numerous foreign ventures."

Candy's brow furrowed. "Didn't you say your family's fortunes were in oil?"

Skip nodded. "That's true, but we don't inherit our fortunes. Each generation is expected to start from scratch and make its own way. Besides, once you make a lot of money, you have to continue working hard to keep it. Dad's worth five million at last count, but I'll never see a penny of his money. I don't care to … Like Granddad, Dad will have a heart attack before he's sixty. His three wives will divvy up his fortune. My brother and I had better have our own starts by then, or we're going to live in penury as oil bums."

Candy's perspective was jolted. She asked, "Do you fear us women because you think we're all gold diggers?"

Skip laughed. "I don't think about the matter. I know you're all gold diggers. Tell me how you'd like marrying a man who's always away on a job."

She smiled. "Actually, the profession I've chosen puts the shoe on the other foot."

He shook his head. "You must plan to practice medicine the old fashioned way."

Candy squinted at her smiling companion. "By that, you must mean General Practice. Yes, I'll be an old fashioned GP. Why are you shaking your head?"

"My family has never had much faith in doctors. Let me tell you a story that might clarify. First, though, let's order some of that key lime pie you mentioned." Skip beckoned the waiter and placed the order. Meanwhile, the busboy came to remove the dinner plates and cutlery.

Skip waited until the staff had left them with dessert. Daylight was fading fast, and the ocean was becoming a mystery in the enveloping dark. "Where was I? Oh, yes. Grandmother never sought out a doctor. She used herbal remedies instead. She was consulted by her peers about every kind of cure. One time, she became so sick she sent Dad to fetch the doctor she had never seen because she was so healthy. Dad told me the doctor was in his own sick bed at the time, but he rose and asked his wife to fetch his clothes and bag. 'If Mrs. Loridge is asking my help, she must be far sicker than I am. I must go see her at once.'"

Candy was listening intently to what Skip was saying. "Your grandmother and I might have had a lot to talk about."

Skip's eyes sparkled. "She's one of a kind, a perpetual student, nurse, and doctor for her family and my dad's family as well."

The pair ate their key lime pie with chitchat about their respective senior years between bites. The waiter brought two checks and received two payments with two tips. Skip drove Candy back along the strip, which was now coming alive with the evening traffic and neon lights. The sun had disappeared, but the dark blue sky sank down to meet a fading, sticky orange glow.

At the motel, Skip said, "Let's take that walk along the shore. It's a perfect night. The sea is calm. I'll give you a few minutes to get refreshed. If you have one, bring along a light coat as it will be getting chilly soon. I'll be wearing mine." He pointed to the line of dunes that swelled, then fell to the flat beach. "Take your time. I'll be standing there among the sea oats waiting for you. Come find me when you're ready."

Candy was tempted to call it a night, but Skip had been good dinner company. She was intrigued by his family. She was particularly interested in learning more about his grandmother, the healer. Multiple thoughts ran thoughts ran through her head as she entered her room, *Man I ate a lot. I need to walk it off … Skip seems to have his head screwed on straight … why not walk with him? I'm lucky to be staying in a cabin next to his … It's like dating the boy next door … He makes everything seem so easy.*

Candy found Skip in the narrow path leading through the sea oats looking out to sea. As he stepped through the sand leading to the beach, she followed him. They walked side by side down to the drying line turning north along the beach, and she drew on her coat against the chilly air. The sound of the mighty Atlantic curling against the shore was a constant rush. They walked just above where the suds refreshed and dried in the primeval, constant pattern.

Candy broke their silence. "What became of your grandmother, Skip?"

"She's still hanging on at a hundred and nine years old. Can you believe it?"

Candy shook her head. "She'll be a supercentenarian at her next birthday!"

"Is that the word for someone who's one hundred ten years old?"

"Yes, it is. My aim's to live that long."

"Grandmother only wanted to live as long as Grandfather did. She curses her fate every day because she could not go with him into the great beyond."

Candy felt a frisson of cold run down her spine with this thought. "But she has the rest of you, and she must have plenty of money given what your grandfather did."

"You are right on both counts, but she married for love. She had only one grand love of her life. She never cared for money. Each time Grandfather came home from the oil patch, it was like a honeymoon for her. So during their twenty-eight years of marriage, she bore him fourteen healthy children, seven boys, and seven girls. Dad was the oldest of their kids. The youngest daughter, Gretchen, lives with Grandmother now and cares for her full time with a maid and a gardener. Grandmother is lucid and always thinking up new projects."

"I'd like to meet her someday." Candy said this without thinking about the implications.

"Perhaps that can be arranged," Skip said. He looked out over the water. "Do you see the lights of those ships on the horizon?"

Candy had been watching the lights far out to sea. She nodded. "I count seven, three going south and four going north. I can tell by the lights' configuration which way the ships are heading."

Skip said, "At least one of those vessels is likely to be in the oil business in some way. Have you ever seen a map showing all the oil rigs in the Caribbean? If you saw their lights from high enough altitude, you'd think you were looking down at a constellation on the water. I've flown in a helicopter over parts of that enormous preserve. And that's only a small patch. For the next five hundred years, oil and gas will remain our primary fuel."

"Skip, have you ever considered the effects of greenhouse gasses?"

He nodded. "Nonsense."

"Pardon me?"

Skip stopped and turned to face her, "I said, 'nonsense.' The natural gas that seeps up from the Gulf off Venezuela is greater by volume than all the seepage from drilling operations worldwide. You'll never hear about that in the liberal media. The only good effect of the media's lies is to keep us O&G folks honest. Yet we're more honest than the nuclear tribe with its Chornobyl and Fukushima disasters. I'm sorry I'm so passionate about this. Sometimes, I want to go out on one of the wildcat rigs and shut off the noise of the media altogether." He turned to walk as before, but unaccountably, she took his hand and walked beside him quietly.

On the shore, seabirds were scared up by the walkers. Gulls winged high then descended to land on the swells outside the breakers. The full moon rose and cast its light across the water, breaking in gold and silver bars of light. In the distance, the lights of the fishing pier were visible above the ocean. Candy thought the pier looked like a giant insect with its stilted feet in the sea.

"We'll walk to the pier, then return." Skip suggested. "What do you think?"

"That's fine with me. The salt air's good for my lungs. I'm glad you suggested that I wear my coat. It's a little chilly."

"Prevention is better than a cure. That's what Grandmother advises. Candy, you haven't told me anything about your family. I feel as if I've monopolized our conversation. That's not fair."

Candy said, "There's not much to tell, really. I'm the oldest of four daughters. Mom and Dad devoted their lives to building a furniture manufacturing and repair business in Roanoke. Mom's dream was to have her daughters grow up independent. She loves Dad, but she had an option with her chemistry degree. She didn't have to get married really, even after she conceived me. But when I arrived, she went out of her career path to raise her family full time. She never regretted it—or never told me that she did. Yet sometimes she looks awfully sad for no reason. She wanted each of us daughters to have as much freedom as possible in a world where women are essentially slaves to men and circumstance."

"Do you really believe that?" Skip had stopped again, but this time he was looking out to sea.

Candy hesitated for a moment. Then she asked, "Can you prove otherwise?"

"Maybe the best proof I can offer is Grandmother. You and she should discuss the matter."

"How many of your aunts and sisters have gone into the oil and gas business?"

He laughed, "All of them have, every last one. The O&G business is like a guild or the old coal mining villages. People who marry into the family have no idea what it's all about. Most divorce out. Some outsiders remain, but their bitterness festers. We've had a few suicides, unfortunately. Do you begin to get the picture?"

"You have to admit that the picture you're painting is not of the fat oil baron with his barrels of cash."

"Nothing could be farther from the truth." Candy could tell Skip was looking at her, but in the darkness, she could not make out his expression. "Let's reverse course and return to the Whalebone. What do you say?"

Candy was a little confused. *Have I violated some unstated rule about voicing my opinions? If I have, I don't care. How am I to know where the rules are going to be applied? I'm beginning to like Skip Loridge, but I don't have to put up with a person who wants to dictate what I think.*

As if reading her mind, Skip said, "I didn't mean to be abrupt or rude. It's late. We really should be getting back to the motel. It's been a great evening. Maybe we can spend some time on the beach together tomorrow. It can't hurt to lie on a towel in the sun and catch rays together, can it?"

"No. I guess not. As a matter of fact, I'm getting tired myself. The final rush to finish exams was all-consuming. I was rushing from one thing to another for three full weeks. Then exam week came. I can't believe it's over."

Skip headed back south, and Candy held his arm. The night had swallowed the beach. The nautical lights in the distance, the moon, and its reflections were the only signs that life existed in the inky blackness of the Carolina darkness.

Candy said, "I don't think it's healthy for you to rule out all women because a few are gold diggers."

"That's fine for you to say, but I haven't found a single woman who doesn't fit the rule. My latest fling was gung-ho right up to graduation day. Then she cut off our relationship because I was going to spend most the summer where she couldn't get a visa: Saudi Arabia."

"I'm not sure I would be comfortable staying in Saudi Arabia, Skip."

"You make my case. Beryl said the same thing. More than that, she walked out on me. We had been through a lot since we were sophomores, and I told her repeatedly what things were going to be like. She never believed me—or hoped she could change things. Now she's gone."

"I can't say I blame her, except you gave her fair warning."

"I did. Believe me. Besides, she had other problems."

"Such as?"

"Such as wanting a dozen children. Such as wanting all sorts of frivolous things before I was ready to pay for them. The list is much too long. She was wasted time, personified. Her only purpose was to teach me what I'm not looking for."

Candy mulled this over for a while. "I suppose she was beautiful and witty?"

Skip laughed. "Yes … and yes."

"I also suppose you acted as if you were already a happily married couple?"

"Well, I wouldn't go that far. She was trying everything in the book to weld us together. If I had had sex with her, the next thing would have been a paternity suit."

"I'm glad to hear that you never had sex with her."

Skip remained silent for a long while ruminating on what she had said. "Well, we never consummated our relationship. That's all I'd like to say. She put around rumors that we had done that—and more. But we hadn't. Anyway, she was a virago, nothing ever satisfied her. Now she's gone looking for other prey. I'm sure she'll find someone who will give her what she wants. Why should I be worried?"

Candy nodded. "Indeed. Perhaps one of your Theta Chi brothers would step right in and take charge."

"That's not the way things get done. She'll have to find another pasture entirely. The bar circuit would be most likely, I think."

Candy brooded on that thought. *I wonder what I would've done after being ditched by Skip after being thought of as his future wife for the majority of my college years. Of course, I willfully kept out of the fray. Now I see why that was a good idea. Three wasted years of a woman's life—and nothing to show for it. I'm glad I'm not Beryl.*

As if he were reading her mind, Skip said, "Put yourself in her shoes for a moment. What do you suppose she's supposed to do?"

Candy said, "Find someone else. Reappraise her life goals. Redefine herself. And you. Could you ever reappraise your life goals or redefine yourself?" She had nicely turned her answers back on him.

He thought about that for a moment. He said, "Honestly, I couldn't. But then … I'm not a gold-digging woman looking for a life-long meal ticket."

Candy asked, "Are you being entirely fair to her now?"

"Are you taking her side in this?"

"I'm a woman. Maybe I can shed some light on what she's feeling. That's what you want to know, isn't it?"

Skip stopped and touched Candy's arm. "Okay, tell me what she's feeling."

"First, she has to be devastated because she lost you. Forget for the moment that the man she was pursuing wasn't the real you at all. Second, she had to realize that three of the best years of her life are gone with no practical benefit. She had hitched her wagon to your star. She has realized, too late, that she was dead meat on arrival. Third, she has to admit that the best hunting grounds for finding a suitable mate are now lost to her. The undergraduate interactions are over. In graduate or professional schools, the climate is entirely different. In the real world—of the bars you mentioned—things can't be good for a college-educated woman on the rebound."

"I see what you mean. But you're not factoring my point of view in your analysis."

"Well, you can start by admitting you led her on. That you're a jerk. That you've lost nothing in this game because you can start over anytime. For example, we're together now. For you, it could be as easy as picking up the next available woman."

Skip said quietly, "I don't think of you as a pick-up."

"Really? Why did you have the temerity to ask me out to dinner?"

"I wanted company tonight. You're beautiful. I thought we could have good times together. Didn't you like your dinner?"

"I liked dinner fine, but remember I'm the one who chose the restaurant. I'm also the one who ordered the food."

"But I'm the one who suggested that we walk along the beach."

"And that's why we're talking about your ex. Confess that you abandoned her at the worst possible time in her life."

Skip shook his head. "That's out of line. She abandoned me, not the other way around."

"I'll bet you could pick up the phone and dial her number. She'd fly back into your arms. Both your problems would then be solved. If you did it now, I could go to bed knowing I'd served you both a useful purpose."

"Things are more complicated than you suppose."

"Skip, I don't know whether to ask you to elaborate or to tell you to shut up until we get back to the motel."

"Well, my three-year steady girlfriend told me two weeks ago that she's pregnant with another man's child."

"Egad. Why didn't you tell me this before? It changes everything."

"You didn't give me a chance. If she was going to run around with other men before I went out on the oil derricks, what was she going to do when we had a family? She clearly had other ideas about our relationship than I did."

"And you never cheated on her the whole time?"

"I did not. I never thought of it. I was too busy working on petroleum engineering and political science. Imagine my surprise when she told me she was pregnant. At first, she wanted to blame her pregnancy on me. I countered that I would want a paternity DNA match since we never 'actually' had sex to completion. She blew up and called us quits. She said she was going to get an abortion. I hardly cared because the child wasn't mine."

"She was willing to get pregnant by another man and try to name you as the father just to get you to marry her?"

"She put the case in those terms exactly."

Candy said, "What some women will do to land the man of their dreams!"

"Tell me about it. Have you ever even thought of doing that to a man?"

"I haven't had the time or inclination. You're introducing me to a world entirely beyond my ken. Lord, how do people coexist when they're so confused and blinded by necessity."

"Candy, you've gone too far. Nothing was necessary about her pregnancy."

"From your point of view, that may be true. What about her point of view?"

"It's no longer relevant. I'm sure you can understand how I felt at the time. And remember—*she* left *me*."

Candy did not know whether to believe what she was hearing. Skip seemed genuine enough, but were the facts of his story about Beryl likely? Even if they were, why did he tell the whole sordid tale? It threatened to spoil a wonderful evening.

"Skip, I don't know what to think. I'm sure you'll sort everything out in time. Tonight, I'm going to have a pleasant sleep. Tomorrow, I'm going to hit the beach with a determined effort to get some serious rays."

"Candy, thank you for enduring my company for dinner and our walk on the beach. I'll be looking to get some rays tomorrow too. Have a nice night. I'll be seeing you. At least I hope so."

Skip went to his cabin. Candy thought nothing of the fact that he had not looked her in the eye or shook her hand in parting.

Candy came awake the next morning to the sounds of gulls fighting over scraps in the parking lot of the motel. The sun was already high as she fixed coffee with her cabin's coffee maker. She slathered sunscreen all over her body and pulled on her blue bikini. Grabbing her shades and taking her coffee cup and red towel to the beach, on the dry sand she spread her towel and sipped her coffee. The blue sea was inviting, but the sunshine was her objective. She stretched out on her towel, face down, and let the sun do its work.

"Don't fall asleep. If you do, you'll regret it."

Candy looked up to see Skip spreading his towel beside hers. He was rubbing sunscreen on his chest and arms. His green spandex swimsuit covered the essentials, barely.

"Thanks for the advice, but I'm sure your fair skin is far more vulnerable than mine."

Skip seemed to consider this fact for a moment. Then he shrugged and ran to the surf and dived into the ocean. Candy turned over and watched him swim. His strokes were those of a practiced lifeguard. Soon he was swimming well offshore. Candy scanned the beach and saw no sentinels. Like the trooper she was, she decided to watch over Skip in their absence.

The man swam up and down parallel to the shore. Beyond where he swam dolphins curled their backs just above the water. Candy saw a dark shadow pass inside of where Skip was swimming. She rose and walked down to where the suds of the waves reached farthest on the shore. Cupping her hands, she called out, "Skip, there's a large fish patrolling inside where you are swimming."

Skip did not seem to hear her, so she waved her arms and jumped up and down. Frustrated by her inability to get his attention, she dove into the water and swam to intercept him.

Candy had a powerful swimming style. In a few minutes, she was in front of his trajectory.

"Hello, Candy. I see you like to swim as much as I do."

"I swam out to tell you a giant shadow passed back and forth inside your pattern. It may have been a great white shark. I thought you should know."

Skip thought about that for a moment as he treaded water. "For safety's sake, I think we both should swim to shore. Don't make any frantic movements. Try to swim naturally."

They swam side by side, angling so their course adjusted for the natural pull of the rip tides to the south. They pulled through the waves and surfed the final distance to the place where they could stand up.

"Thanks for swimming out to tell me the score. All kinds of sharks inhabit these waters regularly. It's not as dangerous here as it is in La Jolla, California. Yet attacks are known to happen. Show me where you saw the giant shadows."

Candy pointed to the place where she had seen the dark movements. There under the water, a dark form moved along the track she indicated.

"That may well be a large shark," Skip admitted.

"Maybe you should spend some time sunning while the great fish patrols."

Skip nodded. He walked beside her up the beach to their towels. They both sunned themselves, taking care to turn over after fifteen minutes. He was on his feet before she was. His eyes were scanning the region beyond the surf.

"I don't see the shadow patrolling anymore. Maybe it's safe for us to swim for an hour. Then maybe we can catch lunch together. What do you say?"

Candy had no other plans, so she said, "Why not?"

They swam back and forth, enjoying the salt water. When they returned to shore, they were famished.

"Let's get a fresh water shower before lunch. Meet me by my Jag at noon."

Since Candy had called the venue for last night's dinner, Skip made the call for lunch. He drove to the north end of the strip and stopped at a restaurant that featured wild duck. He and candy had duck salad and ice tea while they discussed Skip's future life in the O&G business.

"It's the life I was born for. Grandfather's knowledge and connections flowed down through the family to me. Others at Duke wondered what they were going to do when they grew up. I already knew what I was going to do."

Candy said, "You knew the life with all the warts. But it was all you knew. How could you say no?"

Skip thought about that for a moment. "I suppose I could do something else. But I have a theory. Business is competitive. If you want to succeed you have to have knowledge, connections, and luck. If I were to decide to go into banking, I would have nothing to build on. I might be a teller or clerk. But I would not be able to work at a high enough level to make a difference. Consider the problems the world banking system is undergoing now. A teller would have zero effect in the long term."

Candy thought about this. Then she said, "By that reasoning, my wanting to become a medical doctor is a non-starter. Surely, I will have the knowledge. But I wouldn't have the connections. I know I'm not lucky."

Skip said, "Being a doctor is a little different matter. There are never enough MDs. You might not make the top dollar, but you could always make a living as a General Practitioner. Of course, you'd have to fit out your office with high tech equipment. And you'd probably need to join a group of professionals just like yourself. If you haven't sunk a couple hundred dollars in student loans, you could get by with a half-million-dollar investment."

Candy mulled over what Skip said. He was right, in the main. She had suppressed the hard, cold facts. In the long run, though, she knew she was going to submerge herself in debt to get things going.

"It takes five years or so to get a steady stream of patients," she said.

"So you'll have three years of med school, followed by five years of practice-building. You're probably twenty-two years old now. Do I hear the sand passing through the hourglass?"

Candy frowned. "I'll challenge you to consider how long it will be until you have your feet on the floor. You'll be kicking around the industry as a journeyman at least eight and probably ten years. That will give your contacts faith to place significant bets on you. Before you last that long, they'll be reticent. When they place their bets on your wildcat ventures, you'll be hard pressed to sell your future backers on your ideas. That effort will take you away from your precious oil patch. You'll have to make a strike on the first try out. If you don't, your political capital will erode with each failure, with a lifetime maximum of three at the outside."

"Ouch. You're probably right. I'd better be lucky. Outcomes are unpredictable in any case."

Skip sipped his ice tea. He smiled ruefully. "Here we are, having just passed through the gauntlets of our undergraduate educations, and all we can see is brutal toil ahead of us."

Candy made the jump. "And what would we have if we put the two pictures together. I'm talking theoretically, of course."

"Candy, are you asking me to speculate on what our lives would be like if we pooled resources, so to speak?"

"Just for speculation's sake, yes."

"Okay. We'd probably see each other once a year for two weeks for the first eight years. By the time we were both thirty, we'd either both be successful in our career choices, or one or both of us would be a failure. Nothing would have been gained for our having tied ourselves to each other, financially speaking." He looked glum.

Candy said, "But, let's say we were deliriously happy with each other. Further, let's speculate that when we were together, we had wild, passionate sex. Modern media kept us in touch through thick and thin. And on the other side of eight years—"

"You'd have birthed eight children, ditched out of the medical profession and worked at Walmart as a greeter and checker."

"That's not funny."

"It's not fair either. You would have gone to work in Roanoke in your parents' furniture business."

She decided she had finished lunch and their conversation. As they drove back to the Whalebone Motel, she asked, "Skip, is it possible you weren't born with the Happy Gene?"

"What's that, Candy?"

"Grandmother told me to beware of anyone who wasn't congenitally happy. By that, she meant optimistic."

Skip said, "Every silver lining has a cloud?"

"By negative example, you prove the rule. So I guess you're confessing NOT to have the Happy Gene. Maybe Beryl had the same outlook as you. Maybe the doom and gloom that you communicated made a split inevitable."

He laughed uneasily. "That's easy for you to say from the outside. I have to admit; we were always arguing about something. I'm not sure that things would have turned out differently if I had been genetically gifted with the DNA for happiness."

As they pulled into the motel parking lot, Skip asked, "Do you feel like getting more sun this afternoon?"

Candy said, "I'd like to get some sleep. Lunch was great. We can meet this evening for drinks and dinner if you like."

"I'd definitely like that. Do you think you'd like to go to a nightclub and then a restaurant?"

"That sounds good to me. I thought you didn't drink."

"I don't drink. But I'd be glad to have a Shirley Temple while you have one."

"Let's meet by your Jag at five-thirty. Okay?"

"That will be fine with me. I'll see you then."

"Are you going to get some winks or go swimming again with the sharks?"

"Sleep sounds good, but I'll take a run along the beach first. I need to be totally wrung out to get real rest."

Candy collapsed in her bed. She slept without dreaming until four-thirty. Outside, she noticed that Skip's Jag was missing from the lot. She walked down to the beach to collect sea shells. She returned at five-thirty, but Skip's Jag had not returned. Shrugging off the evening as inconsequential, she became determined to have a good time by herself. Yet she waited another hour for Skip to return before she set out in her Jeep to find something to eat.

The strip was filling up with college students who had finished their exams. They wandered in large groups and pairs. They had the wild look of young people on the prowl expecting anything. She found herself looking for Skip among the crowds. On the strip, her eyes scanned traffic for the Jag. Among the wandering young people, she looked for Skip's blond mop of hair. She stopped at the Sea Breeze Bar and Restaurant near the fishing pier. Alone, she drank a margarita and ate a plate of calamari with a glass of chilled Chablis.

"Well, what have we here," a young buck exclaimed as he mounted the bar stool next to hers.

"Nothing that's interested in you. So move right on," Candy said.

The young man was not to be put off easily. "I do like your fire, Mabel! At least let me buy you another glass of wine."

"You heard me. I'm not interested. Move on."

He leaned forward and leered at her. She threw the remainder of her drink into his face. He mopped up the mess with his napkin and was meditating what to do next when the matter was settled for him.

"Look, son, I don't know who you are, but the lady has made herself plain. Shove off." Skip had the man's shoulder in a vice grip. The man was hurting.

"That hurts. Okay, I'll be moving on. The bitch is all yours."

Skip watched the man depart. Then he sat down on his bar stool and said, "You didn't wait. So I came looking for you. It's a good thing I found you."

"I can take care of myself."

"Maybe so, Candy, but the next move was his. I don't think your evening would have ended well, from your point of view."

"So where were you, Skip? I waited until six-thirty before I drove off in my Jeep. Can you blame me?"

"No, I suppose not. I owe you an apology—at least an explanation."

"So explain yourself. Or rather, don't. You don't owe me."

"Beryl called. She's here on the strip. She saw us swimming earlier today. Did I mention she was jealous and mean?"

"I haven't heard your explanation yet."

"She asked to meet so she could tell me what she had been going through."

"You went."

"Yes, I went. We'd been together for three years, after all."

"Did she make her case?"

"She told me she had been to an abortionist. She wanted to get back together, with no strings."

"She must love you a lot."

"She was feeling something. Anyway, she wanted to pick up where we had left off."

"I take it she offered you a deal."

"She said she would be waiting for me when I returned from my year of journeyman work on the rigs."

"That sounds like a good deal, actually."

"It did not seem like a good deal to me. I rejected it and endured her wailing and moaning for an hour."

"So she's gone now?"

"I have no idea. She was halfway on a bender when we met. I suspect she's on the strip somewhere drowning her sorrows."

"Are you hungry?"

"I haven't had anything since lunch, I was holding off until I caught up with you. Should we eat here or find another venue?"

"I've had an appetizer, but I feel like having something substantial to eat, like steak."

He smiled and said, "I know just where we can go for that. Why don't we drive back to the Whalebone, drop off one car and go together in the other?"

Candy nodded. She followed him back to the motel. There in the lot was Beryl, fuming and waiting for Skip. She had a gun in her hand and a glint in her eyes. Skip climbed out of his Jag, and she closed on him flailing her weapon.

"You bastard! I'll kill you for what you did to me."

Candy got out of her Jeep, anxious to avoid what she saw as a domestic incident between long time lovers. The presence of a weapon gave her pause.

"Easy, Beryl. Put away the gun. Someone is likely to get hurt."

"No one could be hurt the way you hurt me!"

Beryl took the safety off the gun and pointed it at Skip's heart.

Skip did not flinch. He stood tall. "If you want to pull the trigger, just do it. Don't play the drama queen."

"I'm really going to pull the trigger, Skip. I can't bear the thought of you being with anyone else."

"I've not been with anyone else. So put the gun away."

"Don't give me that crap, Buster. I saw you with that bitch earlier today. You were like a mermaid and her merman swimming with the dolphins." Now she looked around the lot and saw Candy. Beryl's gun swerved to take aim at her presumed rival.

"Beryl, don't be silly," Skip said.

Candy stood very still as Beryl walked up to her and pushed the barrel of her gun into her chest. "What do you have to say for yourself, bitch?"

"I think I see a woman scorned."

Beryl laughed hysterically. "Scorned, indeed. That bastard ruined my life. He walked out on me. If you were in my shoes, what would you do to him?"

Candy hesitated. "I'd be assessing whether I wanted to kill him or to marry him. If I did the first, I couldn't do the second."

Beryl cocked her head to one side. "Say, Skip, this isn't one of your usual bimbos, is it?"

"Beryl, put down the gun."

"You come and take it from me," she said.

Candy said, "There is no need for violence."

"No need for you, bitch. You have the prize. You stole him from me. I want him back."

Candy said, "I don't know what you're talking about. If you want him, talk to him. Go to him now."

Beryl looked toward Skip. Then she looked back at Candy.

"Skip, come over here and stand by your new flame. Do it now, or I'll shoot her dead."

Skip shifted ground and stood beside Candy. Now Beryl could not decide whether to aim at him or Candy. He took this as an opportunity to move quickly forward and bat her gun hand aside. He grappled with her and seized her weapon. He stood back and emptied the magazine.

"No one is going to shoot anyone. Excuse us, Candy. I need to talk with Beryl privately."

Skip took Beryl by the wrist and drew her into his cabin.

Candy shook her head. She knelt and picked up the bullets that had been ejected on the pavement. When she had harvested them, she went into her cabin. She was shaken and confused. Now she had a face to attach to the name Beryl. The woman had raven-black hair and green eyes. She wore makeup, but the overall effect was natural. Beautiful even when enraged, she had guts and determination. It was clear that she wanted Skip as her mate. She was willing to kill to keep him.

Candy went into her cabin and lay down on her bed. In her mind, she replayed the memory of the encounter in the parking lot. She could find no fault in Skip's handling of the incident. He had disarmed the woman and separated her from the object of her wrath.

That was the second time this evening that Skip had been the hero. Candy recalled the look on the young buck's face in the bar. Skip had not fought him. His personality and strength had been effective in driving the man away.

Candy was suddenly hungry for steak. She decided to drive down the strip for dinner. She thought by the time she returned, Skip and Beryl would have settled their differences. In the meantime, there was nothing she could do to mediate between them.

Candy drove down the strip to the Steer Place and ordered a large sirloin steak, rare with a glass of red wine. Fortunately, none of the male denizens of that restaurant decided to make a pass at her. She was in no mood for that.

It was ten o'clock when Candy returned to the Whalebone. The Jag was gone. Candy locked the door of her cabin once she was inside, collapsed in her bed and slept until morning.

When she was in the shower, she heard impetuous knocking on her screen door. She threw on a fluffy white bathrobe and went to answer it. Through the screen, she saw Beryl with another handgun.

The woman raised the gun and shot Candy in the chest. Then she disappeared. Candy passed out before she hit the floor.

The next thing Candy Silver saw was the glaring light of an EMT light probe. She knew she was being taken by ambulance to an emergency medical facility. She let the EMTs do their jobs. She finally made it to the recovery room after surgery. The physician who had removed the bullet and sewn her back up had also saved her life. A policeman was standing by to take her statement about what had happened.

Candy talked through the events leading up to the shooting. She knew Beryl's first name, but she did not know her last name. She knew Skip's first name, but she couldn't recall his last name. She told the officer that she did not know either party well. She knew Skip only through a couple of meetings. She had only seen Beryl twice, once last evening in the parking lot and again this morning when she shot her through the screen.

The officer wrote up her statement, and she signed it. Then the doctor advised rest. He told Candy she would need to stay for at least twenty-four hours.

When Candy was released from the emergency medical facility, she drove her Jeep back to the Whalebone. The Jag was not present in the parking lot, and when Candy inquired of the manager whether the man named Skip was still staying at the motel, the man told her that no such person had stayed there. A man who called himself Rex Loridge and his wife had occupied the cabin next to hers. He owned the Jaguar she recalled, but he had left the day before having settled his bills.

Candy spent the next five days recuperating at the motel. At the end of that time, she felt strong enough for the long drive home. She checked out of the motel and drove in stages to Roanoke, Virginia. There she was welcomed by her parents, who were astonished by her story of the shooting. Her father was particularly upset by the thought of his daughter's nearly having been killed.

The Silvers encouraged Candace to rest for a month rather than work at their business. She recovered nicely, and by the end of the month, she was anxious to be busy at something productive.

In the meantime, the woman named Beryl Loridge was arrested for attempted murder of Candy Silver in the state of North Carolina. Candy refused to press charges. In the process, she learned that Rex Loridge was Beryl Loridge's lawfully wedded husband. Shown a picture of the husband, she identified the man she had known by the name of Skip. He was, by profession, an oil man, but he had never attended Duke University. She shook her head at her own stupidity and naivety.

The last two months of the summer, Candy worked in her father's furniture business handling product marketing. She used her father's contact list to cultivate business all over the South. By the time summer ended, she had made plenty of money from sales.

When the summer ended, she drove herself to Johns Hopkins to begin med school where the Dean of the medical school invited her to his office upon her arrival.

"I understand you were the victim of a shooting over the summer. I want you to know that you can defer your entering med school if you wish to recuperate further."

"Dean Samuels, I'm fully ready to begin my studies, thank you. I'm still recovering psychologically from a bout of bad judgment, but my physical mending is complete."

"I just wanted you to have the opportunity to wait. As you may know, ours is one of the most grueling medical programs in the world. We don't want any of our students to be at a disadvantage."

"Again thank you. I'll be fine."

Candy did not finish her first year of med school at the top of her class, but she did respectably well in both semesters. In her few spare hours, she dwelled on her experience of the previous summer. She had been impressed by a fictional man with a fictional past, and out of the blue, she had been shot by a real man's real wife. She wondered how she could have been such a fool. She also wondered what her folly might have led to if Beryl had not come into the picture.

Two years later, Candy graduated from Johns Hopkins as an MD. She became an intern and looked forward to her residency. She learned that Beryl Loridge was going to be released from prison and hoped that the woman would not hunt her down to finish the job she had botched.

During the first year of her residency, Candy saw Rex Loridge's picture in the New York Times. His wildcat drilling company had struck it rich in a plot off Cameroon in West Africa. According to the article, Rex's nickname was Skip, and he had obtained a degree in petroleum engineering, with a minor in political science from Duke University. No mention of his having a wife was included in the article.

At the end of her second year as a resident, Candy made plans to open a private practice as a General Practitioner in Roanoke. Six months later, she joined the Shenandoah Medical Group and began her practice.

It was six and a half years since the shooting when a tall, very tanned man walked into Candy's medical office wanting a thorough physical. The man was Rex "Skip" Loridge, the oil man.

"Hello, Candy. It's been a long time."

"Hi, Skip. I don't know what to say."

He looked into her eyes soulfully and said, "Do you remember how we speculated on where we'd both be in eight years? Well, it's almost that long now. I've made my first fortune. You've opened your own practice. I guess we've achieved our dreams."

Candy held the man's gaze. "Skip, why have you come here?"

"I had to see you again. There's been no one else. From the time I met you in Nag's Head, it's been only you."

"Do you know what's happened to Beryl Loridge?"

"She's in an institution for the criminally insane in Straw Hill, North Carolina. Her claims to have been my wife were greatly exaggerated."

"She almost killed me."

"I know. But you survived."

"You never left a note at the motel. You never communicated since. I thought you had just vanished."

"I did just vanish. Until now."

"Skip, I want to thank you for stopping by today. It closes a chapter that has remained too long open in both our lives. If you really want me to examine you, I shall. If not, I've got other patients to see."

"Candy, I'd like to have dinner with you tonight. May I?"

"I don't think that would be a good idea."

"If we can't go to dinner, I'll just have to get down on my knees right here."

He knelt and took her hand. She reddened and tried to pull her hand away. She could not look away from his earnest eyes. He reached into his pocket and pulled out a ring with an enormous, sparkling diamond and proceeded to put it on her finger.

"Oh, Skip, don't do this. No. I won't have it. Please take it off."

"Candy Silver, will you marry me?"

She looked down at him and felt his warm hand against hers. She remembered the hours they had shared together and the trauma of their terrible parting. She began to cry softly.

"Oh, Skip. So many years have slipped through our fingers."

"Yes. But so many more years extend before us. I've got to be leaving the States again in seven more days. I figure we'd have time for a decent wedding and honeymoon before I fly to the Arabian Gulf."

"Are you going to give me any time to decide?" she asked.

"No. It's now, or never. Will you marry me?"

She felt her heart leap up as she thought through his offer and their history. Beryl wasn't his fault, she thought. Then she did something she rarely did in her life—she made a leap of faith.

"Yes, Skip, I will marry you, but I have two conditions."

"Name your conditions, Dr. Silver."

"My conditions are that we have a prenuptial agreement defining the estates we bring to our match. I won't have it said that I married you for money. Second, we wait one year before we marry."

He rose and took her in his arms. He kissed her warmly. She melted into a puddle at the feel of his embrace.

"I agree with your first condition, but why the wait on the second?"

"If you seriously think I'll marry a man I've only had two meals with, you're nuts."

"Agreed, I guess we can get to know each other over technology then, but Candy … I know my mind. I knew what I wanted the day I met you." He kissed her again, softly and with hope for a future.

When she came up for air, she pushed him back and in a businesslike tone said, "Roll up your sleeve, Mr. Loridge. I have to take your blood pressure. And tomorrow, we'll see my lawyer about that prenup."

Hunting Sylvie

Norman Klein

It was five months ago on a brilliant Thursday morning in May that I met Sylvie. I had left the Cape at ten and was half way to Boston when a silver car in the passing lane pulled even with mine, and there was Sylvie smiling at me. I smiled back, trying to place her, wondering if I had met her at the boatyard. Her smile kept us side by side for a little longer and then she passed me, pulled into my lane, and snapped on her right blinker.

I had only a split second to decide. I snapped on my turn signal, and the moment I left the highway the 'me' voice in my head whispered, *What if she's meeting someone else here?*

I waited for her to park, and parked my car twenty spaces from hers. I opened my door, then panicked. I found the broken snow scraper under the seat of my car thinking I would amble toward the trash barrel and see what she was up to, but when I looked up, there was Sylvie walking toward me. I threw the snow scraper back into the car, took a few steps in her direction and then stopped, blinded by the glow of her white shirt and the auburn curls escaping her Irish cap.

"Well, I guess this is hello. My name is Sylvie Hattersley."

"Ralph, Ralph Draper."

"Pleased to meet you," she said, extending her hand. "Thanks for smiling with me."

"My pleasure," I said, shaking her hand.

"Oh, God, I hate this, don't you? I guess this is one of those things that nobody's good at, or is it just me?"

"No, you're right, but we'll be okay if we can just relax and be ourselves," I said, not at all relaxed, not at all myself, and talking nonsense. She was nervous, too, but I liked the way she lifted her chin as she spoke and kept time to the rhythm of her voice with her right hand. We talked for a few minutes, just long enough to get phone numbers and agree on a few things we might like to do together on our first date. I asked her to have dinner with me Saturday evening, but she said, "No, Ralph, you come to me. I'd like to cook for you."

"Whichever you prefer," I said. It struck me a few minutes later when I was safely back on the road that things were looking up for me. I had just gotten a raise, and my team and I were doing the sexiest work on the East Coast. Work was good, and meeting Sylvie was better than good.

***

I had no trouble finding her brick cottage. My rustiness showed again as I reached her front door. She opened it before I could knock and was about to put her arms around me, but couldn't, given my two-handed presentation of a bottle of wine.

"A Cab. How lovely. Thank you."

I got to peel the potatoes and then uncork and pour the wine. The scalloped potatoes took forever, time enough to empty the bottle before we ate.

"Ralph, how do you like my little four-room house? I fell in love with it the minute I saw it."

"It's great. You don't see many brick cottages on the Cape."

"Is it too cute, do you think?" she asked.

"No, not at all," I said.

"So, Ralph, tell me, where did you get that tan?"

"I work outside."

"Let me see your hands?" she said, and told me a man's hands always tell a story, and my hands told her I was a strong man with integrity. That got us to the lemon sole, the potatoes, and a dry white wine. I lit the candles and was moved by the pain in her eyes when she told me she was recently divorced.

"The first year was awful, but I'm fine now, and ready for a walk on the beach or a kiss in the dark."

"I'll pick you up at ten tomorrow morning," I said.

She laughed, pleased, then we talked about our favorite things—foods, wines, places to go, things to do—and then we carried our dishes to the sink and moved over to the sofa.

"Can I tell you about my mouse?" she asked.

"Sure, why not?"

It began with her hearing sounds in the cupboards, and then she thought she saw one, but she wasn't sure, because it was like seeing a shadow, and then not seeing it. So finally she decided to buy traps and set them in the kitchen so she wouldn't have to hear them go off. But the first night she did hear the trap go off, and she just stayed in bed, her heart pounding as she told herself that she couldn't stand the thought of finding a dead mouse in her kitchen. But there was no mouse in the trap in the morning. Then the next night was the same—the loud snap of the trap but no mouse in the morning. On the third night she didn't set a trap, but at three in the morning was awakened by the sound of a trap snapping. She tried throwing out the traps, but that didn't help, and that's how she became addicted to Charlie Chan movies on the Later-Than-Late mystery show.

"I'm no good at being alone. It makes me crazy," she said and asked me to tell her something about myself—something interesting.

"My life story?" I asked.

"No, not your life story, just who you are now."

"I'm a guy who repairs old boats and builds new ones."

"That sounds like fun. Do you have your own boat?"

"I don't need one. There's always one to borrow."

Just before I left, we moved our walk on the beach to eleven the next morning and parted with a kiss in the dark.

I woke up early Sunday morning and danced into the kitchen. Sylvie had me going.

For the past ten years I had been chugging along—meeting people on boats, and frequenting the bars and restaurants that boat people gather in. I was good at the four-day cruises where the customer wanted to impress his new girlfriend and the girlfriend brought along her best friend. I got to know several of those best friends, and a few of the waitresses who took summer jobs on the Cape. But there was something about the way Sylvie and I had met and the meal Sylvie had prepared that told me we were onto something. She was like no woman I had ever met.

Only one thing bothered me. I couldn't figure out why someone as stunning as Sylvie would want to jump-start an old bachelor like me, but I could live with that.

When I knocked on Sylvie's door Sunday morning, she greeted me wearing another white outfit and had her hair pinned up. I apologized for not thanking her for dinner, and she just smiled.

"I have something funny to tell you about last night," Sylvie said as we headed down the road.

"As I was doing the dishes, something my sister told me years ago popped into my head. She told me that before I got interested in a guy, I should always ask myself if he passes the 'abandoned on a tropical island test.'"

"A guy and a girl are abandoned on a small tropical island together?" I asked.

"Right, they arrive in a leaking lifeboat that sinks a few feet off shore, and there they are, the only people on the island. The question is 'What is the first thing you would do?'"

"I'd probably fix the boat. Is that the wrong answer?"

"No, fix the boat, build a fire, or find food are good answers. Falling asleep and then waking up and asking what's for dinner is a bad answer."

I was about to tell her the Cape was an island, but Sylvie grabbed my arm and shouted, "Look, look, there he is!"

"Who?" I asked.

"The green parrot sitting on the hedge. He's our local movie star, and everyone puts out food for him."

We took two steps toward him and off he went.

It was a little cool on the beach but sunny, and we said very little until we came to a sand bar that jutted off in a soft diagonal. We walked to the end and wrote our names in the sand, and that got us talking.

"What's going to happen to the parrot when the weather turns cold?" I asked.

"That's what everybody wants to know. He'll probably go home, don't you think?"

"I don't know. Maybe he'll fly south with the robins."

"What about you, Ralph? Will you stay on the Cape this winter?"

"Sure, that's when I get to build boats."

"That's good. I'll be your sunshine if you'll be mine," she said.

We just held each other for a bit, drunk on sunshine, then watched as a lick of tide washed over our names and realized that our sand bar was about to become an island.

We retraced our steps, took off our shoes, and pranced through the shallows at the end of the sand bar, rolled up our wet pants, put on our shoes, and decided on fish and chips at Fisherman Joe's for lunch.

As we settled into our second beer, I asked Sylvie to tell me about her sister.

"No, my sister died of cancer last summer. I don't want to talk about it."

"I'm sorry."

"Let's just forget the past and live for today and believe in tomorrow. That's the rule from now on."

We tried it out. Sylvie made a list of all our ideas for things to do. I agreed to make her pancakes the following Sunday, and then there was the bird sanctuary, the cedar forest, the Sandwich dunes, and a play in Chatham. I promised I'd take her for a sail on my next day off, then she brainstormed ideas for her next job. She had been offered a job as a hostess in one of the better Cape hotels, but what she really wanted to do was work on a newspaper or at the local cable television station.

We managed to get through lunch without talking about anything but the future, but I told her that it might be a good idea to change the rules a little so that we could talk about the things that we've seen and done together. She agreed that was a must.

"Good idea," she said, "because sooner or later I was going to have to tell you how sexy you looked the other day with your sleeves rolled up and your arms and hands so strong and tan from working in the sun."

***

My sister Winnie called late Tuesday night to tell me that she'd been missing me. I assured her that I was fine, and filled her in on Sylvie and her silver car, and our two dates.

"Oh, my God, Ralphie," was her response, "two dates and you're nuts about her. What's the deal? Is she some kind of beauty queen?"

"No, she's got a couple of scars she hides with makeup," I said.

"Sorry, it' none of my business," Winnie said in her sweet little sister voice, then went on to tell me she had been worried about me because I was obviously lonely and increasingly vulnerable in my own sweet way.

"So, have you talked to Brent, lately?" I asked, knowing that just my father's name would sidetrack her sudden interest in my personal life.

"No, how about you?" she asked. "The reason I'm asking is that chances are pretty good that Grandma Draper left me a nest egg, and maybe something for you as well."

"Maybe," I said, knowing where she was headed, "but if she did, I'd sign it over to you and Gary."

"The point is—" she said, and then I interrupted her saying that the point was that I should ask Brent how much Grandma had left her and when would she get it.

"Ralphie," she said softly, and sweetly, "I really do miss you. You are the only person on the face of this earth who understands me, I swear."

"I love you, too, Winnie."

"So, please, pretty please, will you ask him for me?"

"Okay, but only if you promise to be nice to Sylvie when you meet her."

"I promise."

***

My next day off was Thursday, and the first thing I did that morning was to call Sylvie and invite her over for breakfast, and the second thing I did was to admit to myself that Winnie was right. I was nuts about Sylvie, and couldn't stop thinking about her as I cooked our eggs. The weather was perfect for a once around the harbor, but Sylvie loved the salt spray in her hair and the feel of the wind lifting the bow as we skimmed the swells. She stayed with me until we were both soaked and chilled, then we raced to my apartment and shared a warm shower.

We took a nap, picked out some of my clothes that almost fit her, and then went out for a late lunch. I asked her how she was doing, and she said, "Just great, Ralph. I feel brand new and refreshed. How are you doing? How does it feel to have won the heart of a forty-two-year-old virgin?"

The answer was written all over me. I was loving every minute of it.

We had a great talk about being a couple at lunch. I told her I knew of only one couple who loved each other so much it was immediately visible. They had created their own language of touches and glances, and everyone who met them knew in an instant they were together and always would be.

"I think we made a start on the sandbar, don't you Ralph?"

I nodded, and it went on from there, in the back row of an early show, and then later in a booth at the West End Grill. We sat side by side as we ate, whispering little nothings about what we liked and didn't like about the movie, and then she summed up the plan for the weekend; Saturday night in Chatham, Chef Ralph's pancakes on Sunday morning, and Sylvie's bed after lunch.

"Sounds good to me," I said, enjoying the pleasure she took filling out our dance card.

But what started as a perfect evening suddenly went bad as we left the West End an hour later. As I held the door for Sylvie, a guy followed her out and said, "Hey, Diane, where you been keeping yourself? See you at the meeting next week?"

"No, no more workshops for me," she said, not breaking stride. "Ralph and I are pretty busy these days."

"I hear you. I hear you," he said as I opened the car door for her and she stepped in and closed it. Seconds later I noticed he hadn't left, and when I started the car, he opened her door and said, "Your talents will be missed. You absolutely must come."

"Not a chance, Dave," she said and closed the door.

"What was that all about?" I asked as I pulled into traffic.

"He wanted me to sign up for another acting workshop at the college. He directs the play at the end of the class."

"So is Diane the name of a character you played last summer?"

"No, my legal name is Diane Sylvia Hattersley, but all my friends call me Sylvie."

"He seemed to treat you like you owed him something."

She looked over at me with daggers in her eyes.

"I'm going to tell you two things about Dave," she said, warning me that I had crossed the line by asking about him. She went on to tell me that everyone in the workshop used to make fun of the way he would flutter his eyes as he coached people in an intense whisper that forced you to move closer to him. The second item was that he had told each of the single women in the class that they were on the brink of a breakthrough, and he recommended extended after-dinner exercises and coaching that he promised would move them to the next level.

"So that's who Dave is," she said, "but you have got to promise me that that's the last time you will ever try to hunt me down."

***

The next two weeks were glorious. Sylvie's grace and good looks got her a hotel job as a hostess, and the boathouse got busy as we rolled into June, but we were able to keep to our Thursday and Sunday schedule and do most of the walks and movies we had planned. We returned to our sand bar one morning, and I wrote her name in the sand, and she wrote mine. When we returned to her cottage, she made coffee, and I told her it was the best cup of coffee I'd ever had.

"You're kidding me, right?"

"No, Sylvie, I mean it," I said, and she hung her head and looked away, not wanting me to see her with tears in her eyes, and it was at that moment I knew I was in love with her.

Then came another bump in the road. In mid-June, my father let himself into my apartment with his key and caught us half naked.

"I can't believe my eyes," my father said, "my son has finally found himself a woman—amazing."

Sylvie winced when he said that, and I realized that I should have broken our 'never talk about the past' arrangement and warned her about Brent, his bad manners and the insults he throws my way. Only Brent could say what he did and intend it as a compliment.

"Sorry, sorry, I'm Brent, Ralph's father. I sell art. I've got half my inventory stored here. This used to be my gallery."

"Did you see the way he looked at me with that nasty grin on his face as he said good-bye?" she said.

"Nobody likes him," I said and helped him carry out the eight paintings he wanted to feature in his new gallery. As soon as they were loaded, I told him Winnie had seen Grandma Draper's will and knew that something had been set aside for her. I knew that he'd spent the money on his new gallery, but I wanted him to promise me she would get it sometime soon.

"Tell her I got to sell these paintings first," he said, and I nodded, thinking it was time to change the locks on my doors.

***

On Labor Day weekend, I worked two three-day trips with clients who were shopping for boats, and because the two trips were back-to-back, I had to miss both Sunday and Thursday. I called her when we docked on Tuesday and was knocked off my feet when I got a 'no longer in service' message. I hurried to my place thinking she might be there but found only a short message from Sylvie saying that she had changed her phone number and would get back to me as soon as she could. It was a hurried and worried message. She sounded frightened.

My hand was shaking as I hung up the phone. A thousand things raced through my head. She had been arrested or hunted down by someone.

Thursday morning I drove over to her cottage thinking she might have been evicted.

But her car was there, and there was a BMW behind it. I knocked. No one answered, so I tried the door. It wasn't locked. There was a man's jacket hung over a kitchen chair and a check on the table, a check for two thousand dollars made out to Diane Hattersley by her ex-husband. There were two bottles of Scotch next to it. I peeked into the bedroom just to make sure they weren't there. The bed was made, but there was a half-empty Scotch bottle on the dresser next to a condom wrapper. The fact that both cars were there told me they were out parrot watching and walking our beach.

When she called Sunday morning, I told her what I'd seen when I stopped by on Thursday.

"My ex showed up with my check. No big deal."

"A check and three bottles of Scotch."

"He was trying to be nice to me for once. That was a peace offering."

"Why don't you come over for pancakes. We need to talk," I said.

Ten minutes later she came through the door angrily.

"Okay, so I slept with him. I couldn't help it. I need those checks, Ralph."

"But what about us?"

"I didn't tell him about us. I wasn't sure I'd ever see you again."

"I told you when I'd be home. We had a dinner date, remember?"

"I remember. That's why I changed my phone number. So I wouldn't have to see him again."

"Sylvie, that doesn't make sense."

"Yes, it does. I have a new phone, and only you will know the number."

"Are you done with him or not?"

"That depends, Ralph."

"Depends on what?"

"It depends on you," she said.

"You want me to forgive you?"

"No, I want you to remember all the fun we've had," she said.

"But Sylvie," I started to say, wanting to ask her if her ex wanted her back, knowing she would think I was hunting her down if I asked her that. She was spinning, her voice trembling. I wasn't helping; I didn't know what to say.

"You shouldn't have left me alone," she said.

"I didn't."

"Don't look at me like that. You hate me, don't you?"

"I could never hate you, Sylvie," I said, knowing I was losing her.

"Remember, I was the one who found you and cooked for you."

"And told me not to hunt you down."

"Because you don't have to. I'll always come back to you."

"But I'll never know where you've been."

"Here I am, Ralph. Do you want me to make some coffee for you?"

I Miss You

David Rae

You called again last night. You called when everyone was gone. I picked up the phone on the first ring. I knew it would be you. I was up anyway; hoping that you'd call. I was waiting for your call—if I'm honest. I was hoping that you'd call. You always do.

"I miss you." That's all you said. That's all you had to say.

"I miss you too," I whispered the words and wondered if you could hear them. It's the truth. I miss you more and more. Every day I think of you and look forward to your call. It's all I have left now.

The house isn't the same now. The kids are all grown up and have left. Rachel is married. Can you believe it—our Rachel, a mum? They don't visit too often. Why should they? They're young and have their whole lives ahead, the way we used to.

Now it's just the two of us, rattling about in this big old house. It's far too big for us. We should move, but we can't. Every time I mention it to Alice, she reminds me why we can't. She's right of course, as usual. When I walk through the house, I imagine their voices and laughter. I imagine your voice and your laughter. I imagine our voices and laughter. They were good times weren't they? We were happy. I was happy, especially during that long hot summer. It's silly to think of it, but I always do.

The kids played outside almost the whole summer. I filled up the swimming pool, and they were in and out of the water like otters, sleek and brown. We had to keep an eye on them of course. Some days, we would drop them off at friends, and we would have the whole afternoon just to ourselves. Stolen pleasure; the very best kind you said; just us, all alone together. Sometimes you held me, and I thought you would never let me go. Why did I let you go? I should have held you forever.

You were so pretty. Your hair was the color of wheat straw, perfect white blonde, white gold, and your skin, golden and freckled with little sun-kisses. I kissed every one of them. Sometimes, I imagine that I can hear your footsteps behind me and feel the softness of your breath on the back of my neck. But when I turn around there is nothing. After all these years there is nothing but memories, bittersweet memories that taste like battery acid, or lemon juice, sharp, painful, delicious.

That long hot summer, we knew it couldn't last, and it never did. By late August, the weather turned, hot and sultry, rain clouds gathered. The roses went past, and their petals fell to the ground; red and white petals turning brown and rotten littered the bare ground. Even the children seemed to know it was over. Their play seemed less joyful. They laughed less often, and when they did it sounded false and forced. We knew it could not last.

Only we were blind to the changes. Only we pretended not to notice. Only we kept the faith and hung on to every last second of delight. Only us two were so wrapped in love we could not see the end of it. If it would end, then it would end, we would hold on to every last second of joy and pleasure. We deserved that—it was the least we deserved. It was the least that you deserved. You deserved so much more.

Alice was angry when she found out. You phoned me then, I was in the city working.

"She knows," you said. "Come quickly, I miss you."

I phoned back and Alice answered, she picked up the phone and threw it against the wall. I came as soon as I could. I should have come sooner or told you to come to me. There are so many things I should have done.

"How cliché," Alice sneered, "with an au pair." I still don't know if she hates me or you more. Either way, she paid us both back.

There was nothing I could do to save you from her anger. I was weak, and I should have been stronger. I blame myself for not being stronger, but then …

There's no point blaming anyone. I don't blame you; I hope you don't blame me. You knew I was weak. I was always weak. I told her that I loved you, but she would not listen. She never did listen. You listened, that was one of the things I loved about you, one of so many things.

There was nothing else for it. Alice wouldn't see sense. She said it would all blow over. She said it was just a fling. She said we could work it out. And then she said divorce and lawyers and never seeing the kids. I tried to stand up to her, you know I did, but I'm weak. Alice was right about that at least.

I stood out in the rain. Tears and rain mixed together running down my face as I stood on the bare earth amongst the spoiled roses. But no amount of tears would fix things. It was time to be practical and to settle down. That's what Alice said, and she was right. Alice is always right.

The children cried when we told them you had left. But they were off to school soon anyway. They never talk about you, but I'm sure they remember. How could they not; they loved you almost as much as I did. But life goes on. That's the strange thing. Like I said; Alice was right.

Once you were gone, Alice calmed down. My clothes were put back in the wardrobe. There was no more wild talk of divorce or selling the house, or splitting the business. We even started to make love again. It was hard physical love, dutiful love. A love dried up and with all the pleasure gone; the kind of love that only really deserves to be called sex, but it was enough, for her, and enough for me, at the beginning. But it wasn't real love, not like ours. Not the kind of love that smacks you in the face and takes your breath away. Not the kind of love that lasts forever. Not the kind of love that endures even beyond the grave. Not the kind of love that makes you call out to me from a hole in the ground under the roses every night.

Not the kind of love that make the phone ring late at night when no one else is around. Not the kind of love that whispers "I miss you," and forgives me for being so weak.

Every night when Alice is asleep, and I am all alone, you call.

"I miss you." That's all you say, and it's enough. I miss you too, I miss you so much. I'll be with you soon … when I can find the strength.

Only the Young

Alaina Symanovich

Stepping into the Myrtle Beach heat feels like stepping into an open mouth; its yawning humidity pinks my cheeks and sets me sweating before I take two steps from my car. Sunlight careens off every surface of the parking deck, sheening bright off windshields, peeking over the six-story building, glinting off every bumper and hubcap. I scowl as I heft my suitcase out of the trunk. It weighs almost fifty pounds, all of which work to raze the skin from my big toe as I wrangle it to the pavement.

"Fuck," I hiss at the bag, inspecting the marble-sized raw patch on my toe. Its color sings in the bright sun, cheery as the Small World ride at Disney. Disney—where I would be, had I been thinking straight when my cousin called. I should be at the realtor's convention in Orlando, should never have agreed to this inane stopover. My family's never done the Brady Bunch shtick, never kept up any charade of intimacy or concern. Visiting a cousin—not an ailing grandma or long-lost aunt—without the exigency of death or disaster feels downright foolish. I wouldn't have agreed to it if I weren't the biggest fool of all, nearly dropping a jar of Ragu when Corey called to invite me to stop at The Cove on my drive to Orlando.

My suitcase growls behind me as I wheel it toward the entrance. In fifteen years, little about the resort has changed; its industrial-sized AC units still roar all day and night, loud enough to preclude conversation in the breezeway. The small, dank elevator boasts a scrim of sand and the overwhelming smell of salt. The building's storm-proofed exterior, textured like a slapdash frosting job, is ridged in black. And Corey, bursting out of 501 before I can knock, grins the same toothpaste-ad grin I remember from half my lifetime ago.

"Mellie!" he cries, exuberant, making me feel fifteen again. That voice—always soaked in laughter, reaching me over crashing waves and crowd-clotted beaches. "You made it! We were getting worried."

"Worried?" I furrow my eyebrows, scoffing like someone who hasn't spent a harrowing two hours navigating the summertime interstate. "I hit traffic. No big deal."

"We've got a big barbecue planned for after the baby's nap. Come say hi to Janine, then I promised I'd stay out of her hair," Corey shrugs, wide-eyed and unassuming. It's hard to believe he's a father to not one, but two, children. "I wish I could stay inside during LC's nap, but I can't ever seem to be quiet enough."

"LC?"

"Little Corey. The baby's nickname," Corey winked. "Janine wanted to name him Maxwell, but I said, what? Like the coffee?"

Corey gestures me inside, brandishing a finger at his lips as if we're embarking on a drug bust, not tiptoeing past a baby's room. He smiles and jabs his thumb at a closed door to our left, which I take to be Little Corey's den. Poor thing, saddled with a kiddie name for the rest of his life. Try as I might to reinvent myself as Melanie Connelin, successful Virginia realtor, someone inevitably outs me as Mellie to my clients. I liken the feeling to a waterpark experience when I was nine—whirling down the funnel of the Torrential Tornado, feeling a yank at my bikini bottoms, a cold whoosh between my legs. Call me dramatic, or just concede that nothing's worse than trying to hash out a tough negotiation only to have the receptionist trill over the intercom, "Mellie! Mellie, RE/MAX is on the line."

The air conditioning in Corey's condo blasts like God, streaming from some unseen but omnipresent source. On the shell-patterned couch, hair knotted in a greasy bun and bangs shellacked to her forehead, Janine loafs like an overturned turtle. If I hadn't kept track of her online profiles over the years, I wouldn't recognize her as the bronze-skinned, taut-stomached beauty who'd dismantled my adolescent confidence. I remember an Amazonian Janine: popping out for ten-mile runs in (very little) Spandex, sweat crowning her temples like it felt blessed to be there. She'd been competitive about her Cross Country career, mercilessly so about her relationship with Corey. I didn't understand Janine's Olympic cattiness about my friendship with Corey until Trisha, Dad's girlfriend at the time, whispered that it was "just good old-fashioned jealousy." Which did nothing for my opinion of Trisha the Bimbo or Janine the Bitch.

But this Janine, wearing a too-tight halter that squeezes pods of fat between her breasts and her armpits, and etches each belly roll in sharp relief, looks nothing like the knockout I remember. This Janine looks like she needs Weight Watchers and a days-long power nap. She waves a weary hello at me, then hides her face under a damp cloth. The kind of thing I've never seen anyone do, except in movies. Corey gives me a don't-mind-her shrug and maneuvers my suitcase out of the main walkway.

"Outside," he mouths, gesturing to the balcony. The glass door makes a rumbling sound as he slides it open.

From the fifth floor, we can see miles of beach—the eccentric patchwork that only seems normal because I grew up vacationing at The Cove. To our left spans a two-mile stretch of nature preserve, nothing but pristine sands and a dense forest that houses a spiritual retreat. Early mornings, a band of Hare Krishnas practices yoga on the shore. To our right sits the Myrtle Beach RV Park, an eyesore campground teeming with children who never wear shirts and parents who, apparently, can only hear their radios on max volume. There's a sharp division between The Cove's shore, with its handful of umbrellas, and the wall-to-wall disaster of the RV Park's beach.

"Is it like you remember?" Corey asks, resting his elbows on the thick wooden guardrail.

I nod at the incoming waves. The sound lulls me back to childhood the way the tide pulls you into the ocean, rushing past your ankles and burying your toes in the sand.

"Hasn't changed a bit," I say. "Except we're the adults, now."

"How's your dad?"

I roll my eyes at the sea. "He had a tragic split-up with wife number three. Or was it four?" I shake my head. "Who cares."

I ignore Corey's frown, pointing my head toward the nature preserve. Somewhere beneath the canopy of trees, the Hare Krishnas are doing their Hare Krishna thing. I picture them draped in white robes, monk-like, and chanting, or at least speaking in hushed tones. Even though every time I spied on their morning yoga, they looked just like my family, tinged blue with sunscreen and making normal conversation.

"I miss Trisha," Corey says, moving a breath closer. "She was nice."

I laugh. "You mean her tits?"

As usual, Corey ignores the dig. Happy-go-lucky Corey could never say a bad word about anybody. It irked me even as a teenager, watching him flit between relatives like a trophy everyone coveted. Whereas my dad kept dimming his eyelids at me, a stern, silent question, *why can't you be pleasant?*

Corey clears his throat. "Whatever happened to her? Trisha, I mean."

"Who knows? I'm not the census bureau," I shrug at the horizon. "She was, like, one wife and two girlfriends ago."

"Well, good for your dad," Corey works to keep his voice neutral. "To keep trying, and all."

"For God's sake," I give Corey the nastiest snarl I can manage without turning from the nature preserve. "He's not here. You can ease up on the ass-kissing."

But he just beams at me with that charming grin, lifting his palms up in mock surrender. "Uncle, uncle," he jokes, the childhood plea for mercy. Except we aren't ten and six, and I'm not bending his thumb until his face blanches every shade of white. I glare at him, reproachful. "Mellie. Look. I'm a father, too, now. And I can't imagine what I'd do if Blakely or LC felt about me the way you feel about your dad."

I have half a mind to tell him not to become a cheating scumbag then, but I can't say that with any semblance of moral superiority. Not with the pier looming a mile past the RV park, a shadow on stilts above the ocean. Not when I remember what happened in the shadows of that stilted pier.

"Where is Blakely?" I ask, to change the subject. I scan the beach as if I expect to see a girl lofting a Blakely placard. Mostly I want to look anywhere but at Corey. I remember myself in the kitchen, gaping at that jar of Ragu, hope pulsing its stupid rhythm in my chest. No smarter than I was at fifteen, chubby and lonely and smitten by Corey's smarm. Or charm, as I think of it some nights after a little wine.

"At the pool, there," Corey points to the aquamarine ellipse between the resort and the sand dunes. "Black bikini."

I can't help myself; I laugh out loud. "There it is."

Corey stands, taking the weight off his elbows. "What?"

"Janine," I smirk. "I knew I'd run into her, somehow."

Except the sight of Blakely, her pert, peach-sized breasts, and sculpted legs, doesn't stir the boiling envy in my gut that Janine once did. I look nothing like the girl-woman I was at fifteen, the one who'd watched her body morph from a gaggle of angles to an embarrassment of excess in the span of a year. I entered high school resembling a little boy, and by April couldn't squeeze my thighs into my jeans, had to clamp my chest inside two sports bras before gym. I felt glutted all over; breasts too unwieldy, skin too oily, hips too thick. By graduation, I'd have grown another inch and adopted the gospel of aerobics, but that summer I felt hopeless.

Now, from the way Corey keeps side-eyeing me, I don't feel a lick of jealousy. Especially not with Janine belly-up on the couch inside, the lukewarm rag still tacked to her head.

"Blakely is the spitting image of her," Corey admits. "She's got my eyes, though."

"She's beautiful. She a runner?"

He shakes his head, dumb with pride as only a parent can be. "Soccer. Smart as a whip, too. Third in her class."

A shiver runs through me, in spite of the swirling July heat. "How old is she?" Though of course I already know.

"Fifteen next winter."

Corey must be thinking what I'm thinking. Otherwise, he would have answered "fourteen," like a normal person. I flex my fingers around the wooden railing, watching the veins on the backs of my hands pop.

"If you don't mind, I'm going to clean up a little," I hear myself say, pushing back from the railing. My feet smack the concrete as I stumble toward the door handle. "I won't wake the baby." In this strange moment, feeling the air crackle, alive, I can't think of the baby's name.

I wade through different memories inside the condo—safer ones. I shared a taupe-colored bathroom identical to this one with Trisha that summer. While she did Pilates DVDs in the living room, I barricaded myself inside and exacted my revenge in measured doses—a dash of Nair in her shampoo one day, a pour of perfume down the drain the next. If I pilfered time alone in the kitchen, I emptied her jug of skim milk and replenished it with whole; I pinched bruises in her bananas and spit in her two-liter of diet soda. Eyeing the bedroom, I remember tearing the last pages out of her romance novels on the nightstand, leaving so little damage that they just looked misprinted.

I wash my face and pat it dry with one of Janine's plush mint towels—a neatly folded, color-coordinated detail that screams a mother's presence. In Dad's parade of girlfriends, only a few gunned for the position of Woman of the House, sprinkling lace doilies and potpourri throughout our rooms, schlepping me to nail salons and makeup counters. Trisha tried her best, with iffy results—she slipped me copies of Cosmo but didn't remember linens for our stay at The Cove. Dad bought us low-thread-count sheets that we wadded up and threw away at the end of the week. Trisha apologized profusely, embarrassed that we didn't have nice blankets and washcloths like Corey's family did, but Dad just smiled tight-lipped and said, "no worries, no biggie." That's how I knew Trisha wouldn't last. Dad only criticized the women he had plans for.

"I think you should make an effort with Janine," Trisha said to me one morning, following me onto the balcony uninvited. I interpreted it as, 'you should make an effort with me; you should give me a chance.' I clucked my tongue at the ocean, wondering how oblivious a person could get.

"News flash … Corey's my cousin," I angled my body away from Trisha's Spandex-wrapped tits. She insisted on exercising in the tightest clothes as if she couldn't burn calories without the world genuflecting on her Barbie proportions. "If Janine's jealous of us, then she's one sick fuck," I swore liberally around Trisha, tantalized her with my foul mouth. Dared her to tell my dad and give me another reason to hate her.

"Yes and no," Trisha nudged me with her elbow, and I stiffened. "Not by blood."

She was right; Corey came from my aunt Vivian's first marriage. She didn't marry my uncle until Corey was three. So even though we'd pissed in the same kiddie pool growing up, and vomited together after riding the Tilt-o-Whirl at the county fair, and shared blow-up mattresses until we hit puberty, I could technically date Corey. But until Janine insinuated it, the thought never occurred to me. And when it did, it felt dirty as the yakked-on weeds behind the Tilt-o-Whirl.

Shading my eyes from the sun, I flashed Trisha a cloying smile. "I'm no slut," I said, stretching out the pronoun long and leisurely as a hammock. The muscle jumped in Trisha's jaw, visible as a hammer in an unlidded piano.

Blakely surprises me as I exit the bathroom. She leans against the couch, silent so as not to wake Janine, her hair dried stiff with chlorine. A towel around her waist covers some of her chiseled torso, though not much. But her smile strikes me as wholesome, wide and trusting like Corey's, ornamented by the constellation of freckles on her nose. She looks happy and sunburnt, like any fifteen-year-old on vacation should. And in that instant, I can't feel any more damned than if I were faced with my own fifteen-year-old self. I imagine Blakely, steely-eyed and smirking, declaring, "I'm no slut." Would I slap her? Should Trisha have slapped me? It seems we all deserved slaps, all of us lost girls, that summer, Trisha, Janine, even me. Especially me.

"Mellie," Blakely binds me in a hug. She's all muscle, a snake pressed against me.

I smile, zipping myself inside the persona of the sane, successful businesswoman I need to be today. "Blakely, it's been so long."

"We thought you'd be here hours ago. Dad's been talking about you all day."

I feel the strain in my smile. "He has?" I force the smile wider, feigning softness. "Just a little traffic. Nothing to worry about."

Janine rouses behind us, peeling the rag off her forehead and blinking at the semi-darkness. She sighs, eyeing her daughter up and down. "Clothes. Now."

Blakely trudges to her bedroom, and I lower my gaze as if Janine had reprimanded me. When I look up, she's watching me, her eyes buggy in their purple sockets. "Girls that age," she shakes her head at Blakely's door before shuffling into the bathroom.

You're wrong, I want to tell Janine's back. 'Girls that age'—what did it mean? For me, it meant a tankini cutting into my pelvis, digging red ditches around which fat blubbered out. It meant sulking under the beach umbrella every time my dad touched Trisha. Little things—even a sniff of the neck, a pinch of the waist—turned my mood black. Whatever 'that age' meant for me, it surely doesn't mean for Blakely.

Maybe that darkness is what led me to Corey that summer. We'd drifted apart when he hit adolescence four years ahead of me, kept to ourselves at family vacations and holidays, so it surprised me when his sand-crusted toes appeared at the edge of my beach towel. He cast a shadow over the Harlequin I'd swiped from Trisha's room, the cover of which I angled away from him.

"Hey, cuz," he smiled, dropping cross-legged onto the sand. If it burned his legs, he didn't say so or ask to sit on my towel.

I shaded my eyes, unsure what to say. But he tackled the conversation with ease, firing off questions about school and home, family, and friends, animating me like nothing had all trip. Only after I felt sunburn prickling my neck did I check my watch. We'd talked right through lunch, past the time when Dad left for afternoon golf. As Corey carried my umbrella to my condo, I glimpsed Janine glaring at us from a fourth-floor balcony. She disappeared into the condo before I could show Corey.

The next day, sunburnt and sore, I took refuge in the poolside shade with my CD player. I'm not sure why I closed my eyes—because I didn't expect Corey's hand on my shoulder, or because I did.

The beach was idyllic that day; we alone occupied the pool deck.

"What're you listening to?" Corey stroked a finger over my Walkman as if he could divine the song by touch. My lounger creaked under his weight as he sat down.

"If I tell you, you can't laugh," I said. "It's my guilty pleasure."

His smile crested like the sunrises at home, up north, slow and deliberate and brightening by degrees. Not like the beach sunrises that come at you all at once, like a punch. Wiggling his eyebrows, he said, "I'll show you mine if you show me yours."

Keeping my face neutral, I clicked open the Walkman. *Journey's Greatest Hits* disc revolved to a stop.

"Let me guess, 'she took the midnight train going anywhere'?"

"As if I'm that easy to read," I teased. "Actually, no. I only like one song on here, and it's not that."

He grinned. "Then what is it?"

"Isn't this the part where you 'show me yours'?"

But he just flashed me that coy smile, rose from the lounge chair, and wound down the ramp from the pool. He turned, halfway to the sand dunes, as if he knew I'd be watching. His smile hadn't dimmed a bit.

Now, the sliding door groans open and Corey pokes his head inside the empty living room.

"Red wine?" he asks.

I return to the balcony wordlessly, my eyes on the nature preserve as he pours me a generous glass.

"To our families," he toasts, winking.

I frown at my wine. Besides an on-again, off-again boyfriend back home, I have no family to toast. "To your family," I say. But he stops me before I can drink.

"Bad luck to mix your toasts. How about, to us." He takes a deep swig before I can object. Even before my first sip of alcohol, I feel headiness take me in its clutches. The moment seems unplanned but inevitable. I drink greedily.

"Good stuff, right?" Corey twists the bottle, showing off the label. "I've been saving it."

The stem of the wineglass feels brittle in my hands like one wrong move will snap it. I look at the shiny scrape on my big toe, a bulls-eye that should remind me to be rational, mature, maybe even angry. I hook that foot behind my ankle and drink again.

I don't look at Corey. "Why'd you invite me here?" On the beach below, families trickle across the dunes, spent and ready for dinner. The sun slants in my eyes and paints a long, iridescent stroke across the water.

"To see you," he says, sounding affronted. "Is that so wrong?"

"We're not kids anymore, Core." I keep my voice low, even though I can see that Blakely and Janine are still shut in their rooms.

He laughs—a dull, face-plant of a grunt. "We were never kids."

"Maybe you're right," I say, fingering the spindly wineglass. "What with my asshole dad and his flaky girlfriends, Janine's pregnancy …" I mean it as a joke, but it comes out tragic. I sigh at the few families lingering on the beach. An elderly couple toddles along the water, holding hands.

"You forgot the pier," Corey says.

"Did I?" I meet his eyes. "Or did you?"

And then Janine and Blakely spill onto the balcony, smiling, bearing appetizers like model hostesses, cheese and crackers, and grapes galore. I imagine Janine plodding through the Myrtle Beach Wal-Mart, thinking of me as she dropped items in the cart. Unsure what else to do, I cram a cracker in my mouth and smile at no one in particular. The conversation eddies around familiar topics; weather, sunburns, this year's crowds.

As Janine speaks she leans against Corey, laces an arm around him like a belt, her fingers creeping in his front pocket. He takes another drink, paying her no attention. Eventually, she recoils and pours a glass of wine.

"Not breastfeeding tonight?" Corey asks. I can't tell whether he means to be controlling or curious, but Janine's opinion is clear. She huffs, clunks the glass on the table so hard it sloshes, and sweeps inside. Through the door, I watch her burst into LC's bedroom. His subsequent wail reaches us outside.

Corey shakes his head at me, apologetic, and Blakely looks away. I wonder if she daydreams about her parents divorcing, plans which parent she would choose. Corey, brooding on the balcony with his bottle of wine? Or Janine, with her sighing and her shiny forehead?

The image of Janine stalking away is all too familiar. On a Thursday night fifteen years ago, she stormed away from Corey and me just as bitterly. She'd found us on the loungers by the pool, our heads bent as the Walkman blared on max volume. I'd finally shared my song with Corey, after he pestered me for two days straight about 'the secret.' Such a meaningless secret, yet I'd guarded it like an heirloom treasure. I thought its mystery was the only reason Corey cared about me; I thought if I laid it bare, he'd go back to Janine's side. And I craved his attention, the significance it gave me.

"*Only the Young*," he repeated as if trying out the sound. "Good song."

"You think?"

"Only the young can say they're free to fly away," he quoted, giving me a soft punch on the shoulder. After that, we quoted the song as much as possible, to Janine's aggravation. Every time she asked Corey why he was talking like an idiot, he'd just shrug, wink at me, and recite another lyric. I laughed, even when he didn't make sense.

So the dynamic was already tense when Janine found us mouthing the words to the song on the same poolside lounger.

"Hello?" she shouted, ripping the headphones out of Corey's hand. "Did you just forget about me?"

He tried to appease her, saying something like, "Hey, babe, I was just leaving." But his laughing drawl did nothing for her anger.

"Dinner was great," Janine said, sarcastic. "Just great." She stomped away from us, each footstep like a jackhammer on the wooden deck. I expected Corey to give the headphones back to me, despondent, but he held them back to our ears instead.

"Again," he said.

A flame of guilt lit inside me. "Did you have a—dinner date?"

He shook his head, hitting the button to restart our song.

Later, our parents and Trisha joined us by the pool, toting a cooler full of Budweiser. Since it was the last real night of vacation—with an early start Saturday, Friday night would be a bust—they let us drink with them. Corey pried the caps off my bottles, and I caught them before they skittered into the pool. When my dad asked about Janine, Corey shrugged and said she was in a mood. Only Trisha looked concerned, lowering her beer for a moment and glancing up at Corey's balcony, the only one unlit on the fourth floor.

"Maybe she's in bed," I suggested, trying to sound optimistic. Trisha narrowed her eyes at me.

After two drinks I could do little but giggle, my head feeling like a wad of cotton balls.

"Whoa there," Corey laughed, taking my hand and steadying me as I stood upright. "Let's take a walk, drunky-pants."

"I'm such a baby," I said as we staggered toward the beach. Pretended to sound upset, even though I liked feeling so protected.

Corey squeezed my hand. "You're not a baby at all."

The pier teetered on its stilts a mile away, past the RV park and the strip of glitzy high-rises. Somehow, though I didn't remember walking all those steps, we found ourselves huddled beneath it as tourists clomped above us. Up close, the pier's stilts weren't chicken-leg-skinny as I'd thought, but thick, hulking logs. Where high tide had touched them, they grew algae in green and blue kaleidoscopes.

I didn't love Corey—even if he'd held my hand the whole mile-long walk, even if I wanted him to keep holding me. Love and Corey would always be mutually exclusive. I looked at him as a mathematician analyzing a faulty equation, noting everywhere it erred. I knew him as a ten-year-old, crying over a skinned knee on my driveway; I knew him as a twelve-year-old at the Easter-egg hunt, yanking my ponytail so he'd beat me to the prize. But beneath the cavernous pier, at the lip where the pillowy sand turned slick, and the moonlight didn't touch us, I discovered a new feeling. Tasting the wheaty trace of beer on Corey's tongue, I understood something girls like Trisha and Janine already knew—the euphoria of being chosen.

Corey was cupping my breasts, warm and sure, when he said it.

"I don't want to be with Janine." He sighed as if I alone had led him to that conclusion. And that night I believed it, believed I'd been a cause, not an effect. "I'd give anything to be free, like you. Unattached."

I started to say something, but then his fingers slid beneath my underpants, inside me, and I moaned instead. The sound unspooled in the salted air, a thin, shimmering ribbon. As we kissed, I pictured Janine's face from that afternoon, crinkled with hurt. I understood it, telling myself in that moment that I felt only love for her. For her insatiable desire to be wanted—so human a desire, and something I recognized in myself.

I could have stood under the pier all night, too tipsy to fear drowning at high tide, but Corey clasped his fingers in mine and pulled me away.

"Time to go," he whispered, like we were kids again, helping one another off the tire swing. I smiled at him, bright and sure and unashamed. On the trek back to The Cove, we didn't need to speak. Tenderly, just loud enough for him to hear, I hummed the opening verse of our song. His hand pulsed in mine, keeping time to Journey's rhythm.

"Dad," Blakely says, breaking the silence. The ocean's drawl nearly erases her timid voice. "Maybe I should help mom? LC's really crying." She shifts her weight, left foot to right, undecided if she should stay or go. So wholesome, I think, always the peacemaker, smoothing rough edges, sprinkling smiles like confetti. She'd never mix Nair into anyone's shampoo, that's for sure.

"I'm sure she'd love that," Corey smiles at his daughter. "You're sweet."

Blakely slips inside, fast, as if dodging the compliment.

"Good kid," I say through gritted teeth. Corey studies my face and laughs.

"Nothing like we were, that's for sure." He falls silent, peering through the glass at the inside of the condo. Janine and Blakely remain out of sight; the door to LC's room hangs open, though the crying has stopped. "Go on a walk with me."

"To where? The pier?" I shake my head. "God, Corey, is that why you asked me here?"

Now when he looks at me, his pupils are dilated an angry obsidian. "Is that why you agreed to come?"

"So it's my fault."

"It's no one's fault," Corey grabs a fistful of his hair. When he releases it, the strands continue standing, wild and irate. "It's just reality. Janine and I—happened. And you and I, at the pier ..."

I roll my eyes. "Don't say we 'happened.' Don't say it like it's normal."

I look back out over the water, at the fiery sun streak that slices the waves. "Just tell me one thing. When you made out with me—" I don't bother lowering my voice, and Corey's glance lurches to the door, checking for Janine or Blakely, "no, look at me. When we made out, did you know she was pregnant?" I tilt my head toward the condo, in the direction of Janine. "And is that why? You thought, 'well, I won't be getting any for awhile, so I might as well make a move on my cousin'?"

By now tears wheedle their way down my cheeks, and my throat aches, hot and tight. This, this is what I wanted to scream at him that last Saturday morning on vacation, when I woke to find Aunt Vivian hysterical, Janine crying, Corey refusing to look at anyone. And Trisha, perched behind Janine's shoulder like a Lycra-clad angel, telling everyone to calm down, to support Janine and Corey. That he agreed to marry her, they were in love, he could finish school while she took care of the baby. The betrayal came from every angle—Trisha, who'd known about Janine for days; Corey, who must never have wanted me, who'd taken my trust and so much more; and from somewhere else. It would take years before I realized that the third betrayal, the one I felt but couldn't name, came from myself.

The glare Corey gives me is coated with disgust. "You really think I'd do that?" He clenches his fists. "You really think I'd think that?" Both question and condemnation.

"What was I supposed to think?" I shake my head, imagining the sun illuminating the tears on my cheeks, beaming light back at him.

"So you think—knowing I was going to be a father—I immediately went after you."

"I think you don't give two shits about being a father, or about me."

We are rocks finally struck hard enough to spark. Corey looks like he wants to hit me, and I'm torn between wanting to let him and wanting to hit back. "Says the girl who cared so much about

Janine. Or Trisha—remember her?" He shakes his head. "Don't act like you're Mother Teresa."

I bite my tongue, and the briny tang of pennies fills my mouth. "I was fifteen," I say loudly. "Fifteen! Just imagine some nineteen-year-old taking Blakely to the pier."

"Don't you dare talk about Blakely."

"So you wouldn't like it if some college boy took Blakely under the pier? If he fingered her? If she was drunk for the whole thing?"

With one long, glowering glance at the pier, I stride back inside, leaving Corey taut-shouldered and red-faced with no one to fight. The condo greets me, cool and quiet. Inside LC's room, I hear gurgling, giggling, and Janine and Blakely's downy whispers in the background. The bedroom glows golden with lamplight, and they smile at me as I tiptoe inside.

"LC," Janine coos, "meet your Aunt Mellie."

The baby wags a dewy fist over his head. His lips quiver up into something like a smile.

"He likes you," Blakely whispers, nudging me. I force myself to meet her eyes, working a smile on my face. "Maybe we could take him for a walk, Mom," Blakely says, rocking on her heels. "It's cooler now, on the beach."

"Well," Janine looks from LC to me. "If that's okay with Aunt Mellie?"

I nod, feeling a strange sadness settle over me as Blakely and Janine scurry for LC's things. Sunscreen and a bonnet and a complicated-looking carrier that Janine straps over her stomach.

Blakely lifts her brother inside and secures the buckles. The back of Janine's legs, bumpy with cottage-cheesy cellulite, flex under LC's weight. For all her plumpness, she's still strong. She rolls back her shoulders, looking almost regal; a woman accustomed to bearing a burden.

We don't say goodbye to Corey, out on the balcony; Janine just glances at him, one side of her mouth pinched, and says he'll be there when we get back. We exit the elevator on the ground floor to the whoosh of the AC and trek out the back of The Cove, past the pool with its empty loungers, over the dunes to the beach. Janine doesn't struggle to walk with the carrier, not even when the deep, loose sand covers our ankles. When we hit the firm shore, she turns left toward the nature preserve. Together, we walk away from the RV park, away from the pier and its scrawny legs. We cross the place where the Hare Krishnas will gather in half a day, prostrate on the sand and shut-eyed to the waves' ebb and flow.

Blakely runs ahead, scanning the ground for shells. Next to me, Janine sighs. "Who'd have thought we'd be back here, after all these years?" She's smiling, not at me but at the shore unspooling before us. "I feel like a kid again."

Her back to us, Blakely accelerates, her strides sure and strong as she sprints toward a gaggle of seagulls. They scatter, a cacophony of thwacking wings and angry caws. In the apricot light of the sunset, Blakely's calf muscles snap like flames, flexing and fading in double-time. She sprints to the edge of a gully, one that carves a thick stream from the dunes to the sea, crossing the water in a single scissor. She lands, laughing, on the other side.

"Come on, you guys," she yells as we approach the gulley. "Jump!"

I look at Blakely, her face scribbled with laughter, and smile something like an apology. "We can't," I call, straining to be heard over the waves.

Next to me, Janine shakes her head and gestures to LC. "Not with the baby."

Postal Sex Witch

Kevin Breen

At eight o'clock on a warm May evening, Joe Hanson opens the door to find Shelly Blaze, dressed in an orange turtleneck and tight black jeans, standing on his porch. Her presence—though she told him at work that morning that she was coming—renders Joe speechless. He lets her in and starts to welcome her, but she grabs him, shoves him back on the couch, puts her hand behind his neck and kisses him with her mouth open, and then she deftly—as though she is licking the frosting off a beater, licking it clean—works her slick tongue around his mouth, all the while peeling off her jeans and then her turtleneck. Soon she is naked, leaning back on the couch, her feet on Joe's carpeting, her legs spread. She pulls Joe's pants down, strokes him to hardness, and guides him inside her, saying "Give it up, Virgin Boy."

As soon as Joe enters her, it's as though he has tapped into some occult power; the mother lode, the fountainhead, of sex. He has heard that when you sleep with a person, you sleep with everyone that person has slept with, and, in turn, with everyone those people have slept with, like a continuous chain, or a series of diminishing echoes or ripples. That this is a bad thing—it is the way diseases are passed on. But this is something more altogether. Something rare, and bewitching.

In the eighty seconds Joe is inside Shelly, erotic images—naked bodies in lewd positions, faces twisted in ecstasy, smooth legs spread wide—bombard him. Passionate emotions course through him like he is holding onto a power line of feeling. When he climaxes and pulls out, the visions end; the line, the connection, has been cut. He opens his eyes to find himself slumped on his knees in his living room, with Shelly dressed, heading for the door, out into the twilight.

"Maybe I'll be back in a night or two," she says. "Or three. Or maybe I won't."

The door slams shut. Joe falls on the floor, whispering, "Wow."

In the blurry, pulsing light, he looks around. At his plain gray couch, at the television in the center of the room, at a bookshelf with his stamp collection, at the photograph of his bashful parents on the wall, at the posters of the Orion Nebula and the Andromeda Galaxy on the opposite wall, unable to move or to think of anything other than Shelly, though he has known her for only one week.

***

On the morning that Shelly arrived to work at the Central Michigan Post Office, Joe stood in the back row behind about thirty postal carriers, fidgeting from foot to foot, with a sense of imminent humiliation. His supervisor, David Manning, a stocky man with a head of thick, gleaming black hair, strutted in front of the carriers, preparing to give the annual sexual harassment service talk. Manning told everyone to listen up, and he didn't need any comments from the 'Peanut Gallery.' But as soon as he began, the carriers, male and female alike, shout out comments.

"Slow down. This is a big, long, hard issue to swallow all at once."

"Wait a minute. You're saying that sexual harassment is a bad thing?"

"Isn't it true, Dave, that every supervisor in the post office is sleeping with a worker and offering them special treatment?"

Manning read quickly, struggling to maintain an air of suave authority. His dark hair, streaked with one prominent skein of gray, inspired soft surreptitious chants of, "Pepe. Pepe Le Pew." Manning stiffened noticeably at the nickname, the unctuous alacrity in his voice deflating. On the subject of sexual harassment, he had the credibility of a rutting deer. In the past two years, even Joe knew, Manning had slept with several carriers, granting them extra days off, plum routes, and other favors. When Manning mentioned unwelcome, persistent sexual advances, Joe's heart pounded in his thin chest. He knew what was coming, as it had ever since word got out that he was still a virgin. Sure enough, the carriers shifted their attention from Manning to him.

"Yeah, Joe," someone shouted, "quit coming on to all the ladies."

"You better watch yourself, Hanson."

"You dog, Joe."

Joe's face turned red as if it had been slapped hard, and everyone burst into laughter. Manning told them to cut the crap, but they just jeered louder. It didn't help that Joe, at twenty-nine years of age, had the smooth, fair skin of an adolescent, spotted with large freckles and an occasional painful pink pimple. Beads of sweat, feeling like droplets of blood, squeezed out of his forehead. He wouldn't have been surprised if his brittle, straw-like hair ignited into flames.

When the talk was over, the carriers swaggered back to their cases, and Manning slunk into his office. Joe returned to his case, the metal green sides decorated with the first photographs from the Hubble Telescope, of the Horsehead Nebula and the Jewel Box star cluster, and began sorting his mail. As they worked, the other carriers bullshitted about sports and movies and the lecherous managers at the post office, about malcontent customers and sneaky dogs on their routes, and about who got some last night. Someone asked Joe if he got any last night and Joe felt his ears burn.

The case next to Joe's remained vacant until about eight o'clock, when a new carrier, a woman, showed up. Shiny, auburn-red hair, crackling with static electricity, balanced atop her shoulders. The stimulating curves of her body were distracting even in her loose postal blouse and slacks. The men pointed, stared and whispered, as she settled into her case, bending over to put her purse away.

"Hey, new girl," someone called out. "Watch out. You're setting up shop next to Joe. The Casanova."

"That's right, new girl. Joe will sweep you off your feet."

Joe sorted extra fast, pulled down his case, wheeled out his ten trays of mail on a dock truck and loaded up his mail truck. At nine o'clock, he drove out of the CMPO, into the cool morning air, and was free, thank God, on his own for five blessed, anonymous hours, delivering mail.

The next morning, waiting to punch in, Joe listened to the banter of the other carriers. The new girl's name was Shelly Blaze. She had transferred from another office in eastern Michigan, and she was divorced. Some of the men said that she had trouble written all over her, trouble of the best kind. They all agreed that she had a dynamite body, but a mean debate raged on whether she was adequate in the face department, though, of course, no one would kick her out of bed for that. She had been assigned to take over for Chicken-Bone Smith, who was laid up for several weeks after a hernia operation.

As he sorted mail, Joe felt an extra charge of tension, of impending embarrassment, with Shelly beside him. He hadn't peeked around his case even once, just glancing at her shapely backside when he had gone to pick up his letters at the throwback case. The carriers started up again on Joe, teasing him about putting the moves on Shelly, about his lack of experience. His head stayed red for so long that someone said they should call 911 before Joe keeled over.

In moments like this, Joe felt exposed. He knew that everyone knew that he was a virgin, that everyone believed it was ridiculous for a twenty-nine-year-old man, an irreligious man at that, to be a virgin, and he agreed. They didn't know that he has never had a girlfriend, has never even French-kissed a girl. That he spends his evenings watching TV or going out to philatelic meetings or astronomy get togethers where young women were as rare as movie stars or supernovas. Or, in the winter, on days off, ice-skating on Robinette's pond out in the country.

A heady fragrance, of musky blossoms and hemlock, drifted over to him. He felt someone standing behind him, but he kept sorting letters.

"Hey," a husky female voice called out. "I'm Shelly. Sounds like I should be careful around you."

Joe turned and looked at Shelly, straight on, as if to get it over with. As if to say, "See, this is what I'm like." His face felt hot enough to blister. But just one glance at her cooled him down, like a moist washcloth on his forehead. She was looking at him in a friendly way, her head tilted, like a dog, like she understood the distress he felt from everyone's ridicule.

In some dim way, he saw that she had a similar pain or at least an equivalent hurt in the same general region as his; her eyes looked cold and exposed, but not arrogant, or dense, like the other carriers. He sensed that she could take away his pain, with her mouth, with her beautiful body, like cold water on a severe burn, but that he was powerless to take away her hurt.

"They're jokers," he said. "Clowns."

He understood how, maybe, if you caught her at a bad angle or in a bad light, she could be considered unattractive. She had thin lips on a mouth that seemed a quarter inch too long on each side. Her dark, arched eyebrows suggested wickedness or at least mischief, and her ears were large with little points, or barbules, where they poked through her thick hair. But at the right angle in favorable light, Shelly was a striking woman. Her nose was small and finely sculpted, covered in freckles that blended naturally into her dusky skin. Her eyes were the spectral blue of a gas flame in the morning light. Her head was small and round, her mouth looked soft and generous, like a retriever's. Out of the corner of his eyes, for a second, he thought he saw a phantom border, an aura, of white and blue light hovering about her.

Some of the carriers noticed Joe and Shelly gaping at one another.

"Oh, look, they're in love."

"Jesus Christ. I think they are going to break out into a song."

One of the carriers started singing, "bees do it, birds do it, even sentimental postal carriers do it …"

A week after she arrived, as Joe was loading his truck with mail to go out on the street, Shelly appeared beside him.

"Hey, Joe."

"Hey yourself," he said, startled, shoving a tray of mail to the back of his truck.

A spring breeze blew between the rows of postal trucks parked on the upper dock. Sparrows chirped lustily from the eaves of the post office, over the sounds of the morning traffic.

"Man," Shelly said, "that boss of yours is a horndog. He's all over me. Next time he comes over to my case, will you beat him up for me?" She squeezed Joe's skinny arm.

"Okay," Joe said. "I'll pound him for you. Be happy to."

Shelly headed behind Joe's truck and motioned with her finger for him to follow, to a spot where they were hidden from view. She rubbed a hand, with short, thick fingers and no jewelry, along Joe's forearm, gazing at him with eyes as intense as a blowtorch. "Man," she said, licking her lips, "look at you. As clean as soap."

She pinned him down with a ravenous stare, as though she were going to deflower him right there on the pavement, grabbed his shirt and pulled him to her, covering his lips with her open mouth, giving him a taste of tongue.

"I want to come over to your place," she said. "Tonight."

Joe uttered one word. "Okay." He didn't offer the address, so she had to ask for it. Then she disappeared among the other trucks. Joe delivered mail in a trance, as though under a spell, forgetting to eat his bag lunch, missing an entire loop of deliveries and having to return.

***

For four excruciating days, Joe is so itchy with desire he can't concentrate, but then Shelly raps on his door again, on Sunday night at eight o'clock. Blue jeans and a sheer blue blouse with lace around the edges cling to her shapely body, until she undresses, revealing no bra but frilly lavender panties. This time Shelly takes it slower, kissing Joe, running her tongue over his lips, gently sucking, as though she were performing cunnilingus on him.

"This is how it's done, Virgin Boy," she murmurs. "Kiss me like I am the most beautiful woman in the world. Like you want to spend the rest of your life kissing me."

When he enters her, missionary style, sliding into the grip of that potent muscle, he is again instantly plugged into that voodoo vortex. This time, though, he fights the initial, overwhelming urge to release, and he lasts longer. After the first wave of images passes, he starts to make out individual faces, to identify specific emotions. He sees, or dreams, or imagines—or Shelly is whispering incantations to him—a man and a woman making love. The woman looks like Shelly, younger though, with longer hair, and with eyes that are the innocent blue of a country morning. The man has bushy blonde hair, a mole on his neck, a muscular chest. Joe hates him instantly. The two lovers engage in sexual intercourse in the backseat of cars, on a blanket at night under the stars, on basement couches, in beds, experimenting. From the way that Shelly runs her short fingers along this man's shoulders, the way she kisses his neck and chest, licks his back, he knows that she will do anything to please him, to spoil him, to give him everything she has. And that's exactly how she treats Joe. A fog of pleasure, deep and full and dreamy, begins in his groin and radiates to the edges of his body, to his fingers and toes and scalp, and beyond.

Joe's delight explodes inside him, those good years condensed into twelve seconds of intense ecstasy, concentrated into that syrupy molten discharge. When he opens his eyes, Shelly is dressed and walking out the door.

"Until next time, Joe," she says, glancing over her shoulder. "Ta ta."

The door shuts, and he runs to the window, peering through the curtains to watch her drive away in a purple Cavalier, peering long after her taillights have faded, like stars at dawn. Finally, he leaves the window to face his house, grown quiet and dark. He stares at a black and white photo of himself, skating at night on a frozen pond beneath a full moon, a place where he looks happy, oblivious to all that he is missing. A universe where sex seems as improbable as a cactus.

At work, Shelly ignores Joe, as though she doesn't know him or has no further use for him. Men gather around her case like flies to honey. There are always two or three circling around, waiting with leering eyes, breathing hard, for her to be alone. Mostly Shelly just sorts letters into her case, amused by their presence, but when she is in a playful mood she offers a wink, a lustful glance, or a risqué comment, "Wouldn't you like to know? Do you think you can handle it? I never leave a mess."

Two or three times a morning, Manning struts over, straightening his tie, and shoos the men away, tells them to scram, but then he hangs around, sniffing, worse than the others. The head fly. He flirts with Shelly, makes suggestive comments, asks her out for a drink. The jokes he tells her are so crude—"What do a white woman and a black woman have in common?" he asks. "They are both pink on the inside," Shelly answers, without missing a beat.— that Joe reddens just overhearing them. Even though he's certain Shelly's taste is too refined for a furry barbarian such as Manning, Joe's chest aches so badly he wonders if his lungs are bleeding.

Delivering mail, Joe thinks of Shelly every second. When he whispers her name, his legs weaken and wobble. He adores her lascivious eyes, her glorious body, and even her barbed ears. While walking his route, a half-business half-residential mix on the lower south side, he used to think of his stamp collection, or of the distances of space and the lengths of time in astronomy, of nebulae and constellations and star clusters, or he just concentrated on delivering the mail. Sometimes he thought of the ocean, of the deepest most remote regions, wondering what unknown creatures lurked there. Now he thinks of Shelly.

When he returns to the CMPO, Manning calls him into his office and shuts the door. "What's going on Hanson? I've got little old ladies all over your route calling, bitching that they are getting other people's mail. Four calls today." Manning, coarse hairs growing out of his knuckles, clips his fingernails over a wastebasket.

Joe mumbles he'll do better, all the while thinking, *Pepe, Pepe Le Pew.*

At home, as twilight approaches each night, Joe's longing reaches panic level. He waits inside his house at the end of a dead-end road, refusing to go out, missing this week's Astronomy Club meeting out at the observatory on Kissing Rock Road. He paces in his living room, pours himself some juice but doesn't drink it, turns the television on, flips through the channels—starts to watch *Perfect Strangers* but after five minutes turns it off. When the clock strikes nine, and she hasn't arrived, he crumples on the couch, groaning.

He has lost interest in everything, even eating. His stamp collection, which he has been putting together since he was eight, with his five full books of colorful stamps from all over the world—from Egypt and Kenya and Sri Lanka and Chile—holds no allure for him. Only his stack of astronomy photographs, many from the new Hubble Telescope, continue to fascinate him, but in a weird, erotic way. The Ring Nebula he sees as a giant, cosmic vulva in the sky. The nacreous texture of outer space, smooth and glossy and ineffable, reminds him of the glistening pink walls of Shelly's vagina. The pink Keyhole Nebula looks to him like the folds of the labium. He spends his evenings listening to the radio and looking into these pornographic photographs, pondering a libidinous universe that fills him with awe. The photos, along with the right song—Percy Sledge's *When a Man Loves a Woman*, the Beatles' *Something*—send him to his knees, whimpering.

When was the last time he cried? In seventh grade, when a trio of eighth-graders harassed him after a football game? Or had he cried on the night of his graduation from high school, when the clouds parted and, for a brief and brutally clear moment, he saw his lonely future?

When Shelly does show up again, this time dressed in a black dress, nylons, and gloves, he leaps from the couch. She permits him to run his hands over her body, to place his lips on her lovely breasts, to pull up her dress, revealing her garter belt. She doesn't look at him, stares away at nothing in particular. He enters her from behind, while she is on all fours, and again he connects, inexplicably, to that other world. Almost immediately, as through a skylight, he sees the man with the mole on his neck in bed with another woman, naked, laughing, fucking her. The woman changes from a busty brunette to a petite blonde to a thin, long-legged redhead. Shelly doesn't move or moan at all, just kneels there, rigid, like a coffee table.

Confused, he finishes, pulls out of Shelly and opens his eyes. A dirty, depleted sunset gleams around the curtain edges. The scent of uneaten fish from dinner hangs in the affronted air. Shelly is dressed and heading for the door, but he cries out, "Wait."

She stops and glares. He gives her an imploring look like he wants to help.

"What did you think?" she snaps, her eyes the icy blue of absolute zero. "That it was all fun and games? All clouds and flowers and bunny rabbits? Not in my world. Not by a long shot."

She walks out the door and drives away, leaving him on the floor. He can't catch his breath, unable to get air past the lump in his throat.

Shelly invades Joe's bloodstream, like a virus. He stumbles around heavily, lugubriously, as though he is on a different planet with double the gravity, or like his work boots weigh a hundred pounds each. His ten-mile walking route seems endless. She loiters everywhere inside him, in the nucleus of each cell, like a systemic infection. He knows, already, that he will never get her out of his system. She will be there always, like certain diseases.

When he isn't working, he sits on his couch, staring at intimate photographs of deep space, of remote corners of the universe, beautiful and frozen, until they embody, each one, some small, glimmering facet of Shelly.

He can sense the beginnings of psychosis contaminating his mind.

At work, Shelly continues to ignore him, like he is a little something on the side that she doesn't care to acknowledge in public. Other men come around, like wild dingoes, hitting on Shelly, especially David Manning. Joe smells Manning's assertive aftershave, hears the snarl of his low voice, whispering, "I can make your life easier for you, I can get you any day off you want, get you on a nice mounted, suburban route."

A long week passes before Shelly comes over again, showing up at his front door with heavy make-up—blue eye mascara, dark berry lipstick, crimson fingernails—and dressed in a red leather coat and black boots. Her hair, pulled back, exposes her chiropteran ears. Inside, she takes off the coat, naked except for the boots, revealing brazen tits, a shaved cunt. She orders him to take off his clothes, and he obeys, and she pushes him down on his carpet. She mounts him, backward, and begins to ride him. As soon as she has taken him inside her, he sees Shelly fucking a man, but not the man with the mole on his neck. He witnesses Shelly opening her mouth or spreading her legs for many different men, in dark houses and cheap hotels, in bathrooms and closets and on kitchen tables, outdoors behind buildings or in cars. Some of the men are complete strangers, some are other women's husbands, some are bosses and supervisors at work. The thrill of illicit sex collides with the hard spank of shame. Crude emotions spark through him—lust, anger, desire, violence, revenge. Joe wants to pull out, to end the assault, but she grips him tight as a clamp. The images continue, and Joe's arousal gives way to numbness. Shelly reaches orgasm two maybe three times, moaning, like a virile animal, and then Joe comes, and she rises up off of him and lies down, spent, on the carpet.

The world returns reluctantly; the bleat of a horn, the inarticulate barking of some mongrel, the absurd shapes of furniture in the sullied light, the burnt rubber odor of fornication. Shelly crawls up to Joe and rests her head on his shoulder, panting. She lays a hand on his stomach. He puts an arm around her, patting her damp back.

Shelly's breathing slows down. The beam from the headlights of a car moving down the road slides across the living room.

"Talk," Shelly says, in a disembodied voice. "Anything."

His heart beats faster, and his mind goes blank until his eyes rest upon the photograph of his parents. Even in the darkness, he can see his father with wavy blonde hair parted in the middle, glasses, and a churchy smile; his mother with gray-black hair, a wry smile, looking prim and already old-maidish at forty-three. "My father never told me much about girls. I'm not sure he knew much. My mother never really hugged me. I never saw them kiss in front of me. I guess the real mystery is how they had me. But my brother seemed to do okay. He's married, with a daughter."

As he spoke, he grew alarmed. What was he babbling about?

"All the space pictures?" she says, her eyes still closed, her voice sounding spaced out. "What's that about?"

He believes that if he can describe it just right—the beauty, the spiritual dimension, the infiniteness—he will be explaining himself to her, but he rushes his answer, gets too serious, too flowery, and he can sense the first fibers of this fragile mood begin to unravel. He can feel her start to stir, to awaken, getting ready to bolt. So, he asks, lightly stroking her moist arm, his voice calm so as not to spook her, "Tell me about your family."

She doesn't move for a few moments, and he thinks maybe she has fallen asleep. But then she speaks, her voice weary and sad, like an oboe. Her mother, a tall, beautiful woman, with the soul of an artist, left when Shelly was three. About five years ago, she returned, and they have been getting to know each other, slowly. Her father, a big, tough hombre, an outdoor guy, a hunter and a drinker, rugged and as handsome as the devil, raised her and her little sister. He brought a lot of women home with him.

"He yelled at them, and they yelled back," Shelly says. "My sister and I were awakened many times at two or three in the morning, my father calling them tramps or whores or worthless, them calling him a mean, heartless fucker. He didn't beat us, but my sister and I got out of there as quick as we could."

Her eyes, open now, look glassy and blurry. A loud noise, an abrupt movement by him, might knock her out of this shallow spell. She tells him about her daughter, Natalie, nine-years-old, who lives with her ex-husband's parents. An irresistible idea blooms inside him; that he and Shelly could come to know one another, that they could share their deepest feelings, maybe even spend afternoons at the zoo with Natalie. But then she rouses. Her eyes focus. She looks at Joe with confusion and then derision, gets up from the floor and grabs her coat and puts it around her to leave. Joe whispers that he loves her, that she is beautiful.

She scoffs, opens the door. "I'm a complete frigging mess, you idiot."

"Did you enjoy being with those other people?"

She shakes her head. "You figure it out, Star Boy."

The door slams and he gets up and watches her drive away, the taillights looking like the Doppler shift of the departing universe. He thinks of what Shelly has said, trying to connect the dots of her life, like stars in a vague constellation. What he decides, is that she both loves and hates her cataclysmic past. Just as he both loves and hates his solitude.

The next morning Joe sorts slowly into his case. Shelly has the day off, and he wonders what she's doing. Is she out with someone from work, or maybe prowling the malls or the movie theaters or the bars, looking for a new thrill. To sooth his mind he thinks of her at home, cleaning the house or apartment, hanging laundry out on a clothesline, sewing, baking pies.

The other carriers hardly exist for him. Their conversations sound far away, and he cares so little about what they say and think, their stupid opinions, that they might as well be cartoon characters. He hears his name, over and over, first faintly and then louder, and realizes someone is asking him if he got any last night. He just keeps sorting.

As he delivers his route, Joe thinks about Shelly, wishing she would visit him again. Back in the office, he learns that next week she will be re-assigned to another route, at an associate office across town. On her last day, he watches for her to be alone. Finally, as she is loading up her mail truck, he walks over and stands in front of her, his hands jammed into his pockets. He squints across the dock to the river, the sun glancing off the dark water.

"I'd like to see you again," he says. "I'd like to take you out, for dinner."

She stops loading her truck and shakes her head. "I'm not that kind of girl. I don't hang around for long."

"Does that mean I won't see you again?"

She pulls down the door to the back of the truck. "You're catching on."

He follows her to the door of her truck. "Just answer me this. Why me?"

"I've never had a twenty-nine-year-old virgin before."

He knows he should just walk away, but he goes one step further. "I do have something to offer you," he says. "I will treat you like a goddess."

She looks horrified. "God, no."

She hops into the truck and drives away.

Throughout the rest of the summer, Joe delivers his route in a daze, goes home and sits on the couch and stares at the wall, as though he has some exotic disease. He looks up her name in the phone book and then calls information, but there is no listing for Shelly Blaze. One afternoon, he goes into the supervisor's office and asks Manning for her number, but Manning, eating a donut, says that's private information, and that he isn't the first to ask.

"Did you send her out?" Joe asks. "Because she wouldn't be your girl?"

Manning gives him a cocky grin. "You poor lovesick boy. Not in the least. Now get back to work."

Joe looks him in the eye. "Pepe. Pepe Le Pew."

On late afternoons that summer, Joe drove around the city in his Maverick, through residential neighborhoods, past apartment buildings, looking for Shelly's purple Cavalier. He can't decide if she was the nicest woman he has ever met, or the cruelest. Sometimes, when he is driving, he gets confused and forgets who or what he is looking for, only that he is searching, and he imagines he is looking for deep space objects, comets or quasars or pulsars. He hears rumors that Shelly is working at the Northeast Station, as a secretary, with weekends off. One afternoon he thinks he sees her walking into a bar in a backless dress, with one of David Manning's hairy paws on her neck; he waits in the parking lot for hours, but he never sees them come out.

He always makes certain he is home at eight. Because there is still a chance that she will return.

She does, one last time. She shows up at his door on a hot evening, wearing a thin yellow sundress and sandals. A daffodil adorns her hair. She sits outside on the porch swing, her legs crossed demurely, while Joe leans on the railing and they talk about the weather, about the solar system and the movement of the sun. Joe sits beside her and kisses her on the swing until the sun goes down.

They move inside, where Joe unbuttons the top three buttons of her dress and runs his hands over her lovely body. He whispers as he slips off her panties, that he adores her. He leads her into his bedroom, still light enough to see the luminous posters of the Orion Nebula, the Trifid Nebula, and he lays her back on his bed. When he enters her, there are no visions, just his own thoughts and dreams, which he imparts to her with words, caresses, kisses. He tells her that he wants to make love to her in every room in his house, in every possible way, in hotel rooms from here to Florida, from Maine to California, in the mountains at twilight, in the desert in the morning, under a full moon on a balcony beside the sea, beside a flowing river in the middle of the grasslands, in Paris and London and Barcelona, and when it feels too good, as though he is going to disintegrate into a million tiny pieces, he thinks of his stamp collection, of every single stamp he owns, and then he thinks of every image in outer space, because he wants to hold off for as long as can, he wants it to last, because she feels so good moving underneath him, her eyes the glowing blue of stardust, of the heavens, and he doesn't want this to end.

He doesn't ever want it to end.

Ring Dings

Vincent Salvati

As I awoke from another nightmare, a recurring torment where I am almost smothered to death in one fashion or another, I found myself staring at the LED display next to the bed. 2:32. I tried to shake the feeling of almost dying. It didn't seem to matter if I took a sleeping aid or not, the dreams persisted.

Sliding out of bed, I tried not to wake Barbara. I looked at her with no feeling at all. I didn't despise her, but I certainly didn't like her. We made all the efforts of a couple married twenty-five years. After our third, and final, child had moved out, we were left with each other, two strangers, roommates, wondering what had happened.

I made my way across the room and silently closed the door behind me. The shag felt soft under my feet. When I got to the kitchen, I opened the cabinet door and surveyed the inventory— peanuts, Ritz crackers, beef jerky, Ring Dings, Fritos. I grabbed a pack of the Ring Dings and walked to the back door. Standing there with my creme filled chocolate dessert in my hands, I took stock of the back yard. The moon was extra bright, and things seemed very vibrant. The potted plants on the patio, the evenly spaced Tiki torches and the lawn furniture lined up like it was Club Med, all Barbara's doing.

Sliding the heavy glass door to the right, I stepped into the summer night heat. Even at that late hour, the Arizona air was dry and hot and still. I walked across the deck, down two steps to the brick patio, and then to the edge where the brick met the grass. I noticed it could use a cut and made a mental note to take care of it. Hearing a noise to my right, I glanced over the low fence to the neighbor's yard and spotted Jenny. She and her girlfriend had moved in about two years ago. Jenny, the older of the two, was twenty-eight. She was thin and short, about five-foot-five and had dark curly hair to her shoulders. She didn't necessarily look like a lesbian.

I walked to the fence, and she glanced over giving me a wave. She was on her knees digging with a hand shovel. She had workout shorts on, and her t-shirt was sliding away from her waist as she bent closer to the ground. Her calves were extended behind her and perfectly curved, ending at her white ankle socks and orange Nike sneakers. I just stood there and watched her as she tapped the dirt around a freshly planted shrub. Once it was in, she stood up and walked over to me.

"Hi, Walter," she said, speaking in a low tone.

"Hey, Jenny. Whatcha doing?" *Stupid question*, I thought to myself. I could perfectly well see what she was doing.

"Just some gardening. I like planting at night. So much cooler and more peaceful."

The sweat beaded on her forehead. Her t-shirt had a picture of a zombie and the words I Want To Eat You. She had no bra on, and her small breasts pushed against the fabric. I watched as a drop of sweat ran down next to her eye and over her cheek leaving a glistening trail.

"Yeah," I agreed. "It's a very pleasant night."

"So, what are you doing out here?" she asked.

"I couldn't sleep. Figured I'd get a snack and some air." I lifted my hands showing her the cellophane-wrapped snack.

"How's Barbara?" She asked.

"She's good, still sleeping."

We stood in silence for a moment.

"Do you have big plans for the flower garden?" I asked.

"I'm going to put in a new cactus plant over there." She pointed with the hand shovel she still was holding. Some of the dirt flew in the direction she was pointing.

"That'll be nice. Will you plant that at night too?"

"Probably. It'll have to be a good moon night."

I looked at her wondering what she meant. "Oh, you mean a lot of moonlight."

"Yes."

"Must be hard to see what you're doing," I said. "Hey, I have a set of halogen lamps in the garage. You're welcome to use them."

"Thanks, Walter. But I prefer the dark."

I nodded. We stood in silence again. I was fidgeting with the cellophane wrapper. I held the package up.

"Want one of my Ring Dings?"

She smiled. "No thanks."

A plane flew overhead, and we both looked up.

"Seems like more planes all the time," she said.

"Yeah. I think they're changing the flight routes."

"Oh." Another moment passed. "Well, I better get back to it."

"Okay," I said.

"Tell Barb I said hi."

"Will do. Maybe I'll run into you again when you plant the cactus."

"Maybe."

I watched her as she walked back to the shrub. Then I sat in one of the lounge chairs, folded it all the way back, and stared at the night sky. The only sound was Jenny digging behind me, her shovel breaking the soil. Closing my eyes, I drifted. I could hear the sound of the dirt being tossed into the empty hole. Drifting further. The soil covering me. Being tossed on my waist. Drifting even further, I could feel the weight. Then it was on my chest. Larger shovels full of dark, damp earth covered my torso, and then my thighs and lower legs and then my feet. Everywhere. I could feel Jenny's soil covering me. Another one on my chest. It began sliding to my face. I could taste the richness of the dirt, the grit. Then more slid over that and trickled into my nostrils. The scent was musty and stagnant and brought me back to my grandmother's living room. The next batch made it to my eyes. Thick and blinding, the moonlight hitting my eyelids was gone. All was lost to the darkness. My ears were full of soil, but I could still hear Jenny's shovel digging in the dark. I couldn't breathe anymore. The rich dirt was sitting in my throat. My nose was covered. My whole body could feel the weight pressing down.

"Walter," Jenny said, her hand on my arm.

I jumped, startled.

"Sorry," I said.

"You looked like you were hyperventilating."

"Oh, I must have fallen asleep and had a dream."

"A nightmare seems more like it."

"I guess so."

She took her hand off my arm and sat in the next lounge chair.

"You feel like talking about it?" she asked.

"I don't remember what it was," I lied.

"You want me to sit with you?"

"I don't want to take you away from the garden."

"Nonsense. How about one of those Ring Dings?"

I tore open the package and slid one of them out and into her hand. The chocolate had already begun melting in the heat and took some effort to get it out, but Jenny didn't seem to notice. She took a bite. "So, are you feeling any better?"

"I think so," I replied.

"Look at all those stars," Jenny said, her head tilted back.

I admired her long neck and then followed her eyes to the sky.

"Beautiful."

"So many stars," she said. "So many possibilities."

Jenny took another two bites leaving her with melted chocolate on her fingers.

"I better get back to the garden," she said.

"Of course," I replied. "Have a good night."

She turned back for a moment. "I enjoyed the Ring Ding, Walter. Let's do this again."

I watched her walk back to her yard as she went around the fence. She didn't look back, but I think she knew I was watching her. Then I got up and walked to the house. I slid the glass door shut and stood watching Jenny from the coolness of the kitchen. I could barely make out her shadowed shape in the night, but I watched just the same.

The sound of running water through the pipes told me Barbara was up using the toilet. The floor creaked as she got into bed, and I coaxed myself back to her side. As I closed my eyes and drifted off to sleep, I could still smell Jenny's fragrant soil.

Summer Heat

Destiny Eve Pifer

Haven Sinclair drove along the rocky coast enjoying the smell of the ocean. The air was fresh and salty, something she most certainly wasn't used to. It had been ten years since she last vacationed and that was a trip to Atlantic City with a bunch of senior citizens. Now she was headed to a posh resort for the summer.

For Haven, the last few years had been spent working in a dirty factory with dirt caked under her fingertips. The fumes alone made it heard to breathe. When the opportunity for a vacation came up, she gladly took it. Just a short distance ahead she could see the beautiful resort. Just the mere sight of it took her breath away.

As she settled in, she couldn't help but notice the happy 'in love' couples and began to wonder if she booked the wrong trip. It seemed that she was the only single woman there. However, she didn't let it bother her. This was her chance to kick back and relax, and she wasn't about to let anything stand in her way.

After taking a brief nap, she headed outside to explore the gardens. There was a pool with a waterfall and golf courses filled with avid golfers. In the distance, she could see tennis courts and a workout area. As she studied the workout area, she began to wonder if perhaps it was time to get in shape. Her life was often so chaotic that she didn't have time to jog or workout.

The next day she decided to take the plunge and sign-up. She took a glance in the mirror to study her workout attire and noticed the bulge that was her stomach. Tying back her long brown hair she continued to get ready before rushing off to the class that would soon begin.

As she entered the workout area, she couldn't help but notice that everyone else seemed to be toned and in shape. Suddenly she began to feel a bit self-conscious over how she looked. She had let herself go, and it showed. She was about to hop on a treadmill when a man's voice caught her by surprise.

She turned around and noticed the most gorgeous man she had ever seen standing in front of the room. He was muscularly built, with his upper arms covered in tattoos. He ran his hand through his thick brown hair then called everyone to the front.

For a moment she didn't think she could move. She most certainly wasn't sure if she could work out in front of such a handsome guy who made her heart flutter. Silently she crept to the back of the class praying that he wouldn't see her.

"Alright, listen up class! My name is Demetri, and I am one of your instructor's. Today we will be learning the basics but don't think I am going to go easy on you," he said, pacing back and forth. His voice was rough and stern, but still, she quivered inside. As he paced, she continued to hide in the back of the room. When he called everyone to find a place she hid behind a couple who couldn't stop holding hands.

Suddenly, a beautiful woman emerged from the doorway and joined Demetri in the front. She introduced herself as Jennifer and announced that she would be assisting Demetri with the class.

When Haven saw them smile at one another, she began to wonder if perhaps there was more to the whole workout partner's thing.

"I can't dwell on it," she muttered to herself. It had been years since Haven had even been on a date. Years since a man had even looked her way. As she looked around the class, she found herself yearning for that kind of affection.

"Alright class let's start with fifty jumping jacks!" shouted Jennifer.

Fifty, Haven thought to herself. Just doing fifty was going to be a challenge but she stuck with it. She could feel her legs going weak and heart pounding against her chest.

Just then Demetri began walking around the room. He kept pushing the class to keep going until they reached fifty, but Haven didn't make it before collapsing to the ground. She watched as he walked over and helped her to her feet. She was immediately embarrassed as other's stopped and stared. Haven could feel his strong hands on her flesh and began to shiver. She took a quick glance at his dark blue eyes and felt as though her legs were turning to jello.

Quickly apologizing, she promised to keep on going with the class despite his assistance that maybe she should sit down. The hour long class seemed to drag on and on but just being able to catch glimpses of the handsome instructor kept her going.

Though covered with sweat, she decided to introduce herself. He was talking to a few other's, so she patiently waited. Then as he grabbed his gym bag, she quickly walked up beside him.

"Hi, my name is Haven Sinclair," she said extending her sweaty palm.

He looked up and gave her a smile. "Demetri Walker," he said taking hold of her hand. His kind smile made her heart pound even more.

"I'm from Roseburg, Oregon, where are you from?" she asked trying to think of more questions to ask him.

"Portland," he said picking up his bag and giving her a quick smile.

Just as she was about to ask more questions, Jennifer popped up beside him. "We're going to be late for lunch," she said in a cheerful manner.

With that Demetri told her to have a nice day and proceeded to follow Jennifer out the door. It was at that moment that Haven's heart sank. Clearly, they were an item, and she silently cursed herself for even trying to get to know him. The next day Haven skipped the workout class because she knew she wouldn't be able to focus.

She was going to check out the pool when she ran into a shirtless Demetri heading her way. Just the mere sight of him made her quiver. It was a feeling she never had in her life. Despite the fact that she had dated a lot of men, not one had ever made her feel such passion. She wondered what it would be like to lay in his arms. To feel his touch and warmth. She wanted so badly to talk to him and get to know what his life was like, but instead, they exchanged a simple hello.

Every glimpse she had of Demetri made her heart jump. She was captivated by him and looked forward to seeing him every day. Though she was no longer in the work-out classes, she remained determined to stay in shape.

One day, she spotted him practicing some martial arts moves and waited until he was alone then approached him. "I was wondering if you could help me learn some self-defense moves," she said.

He looked up at her and wiped the sweat off of his face. "Yeah sure," he said grabbing a towel to finish wiping off the sweat. "When do you want to start?"

At that moment she felt her knees starting to shake. "Now if you have the time," she said, half expecting him to say no. Much to her surprise he gave her a smile and motioned for her to come closer.

He began showing her some basic moves then grabbed her from behind. Though she was supposed to get away from him, she didn't want to. His large muscular hands held her in a tight grip as his body was pressed up against her. She could feel his breath on her neck, and it made her quiver. After hesitating for a few seconds, she finally fought back and used the moves that he had showed her.

After his leg had swiped across the floor knocking her on her butt, she began to laugh. Before she knew it they we were both laughing. Just sitting and staring at each and laughing. Finally, he rose to his feet and lent her a hand. With their bodies just a few inches away from each other she could feel the heat radiating off of his. She wanted so badly to reach out and trace her fingers across his body.

As she looked into his deep blue eyes, she was mesmerized. They stared at each other for a few minutes before he got in close to her and gently brushed back a few strands of hair. His soft caress across her face left her wanting more.

As if he were sensing that feeling, he learned and kissed her softly on the lips. Soon their bodies were entwined as the passion between them exploded. However, at that moment he pulled away.

"I think we are moving way too fast," he said.

Though she longed for the kissing to continue, she knew he was right.

For the next two days she didn't see Demetri, and it made her heart sink. *Why is he avoiding me?* She was desperate for his touch but knew deep down that maybe he was avoiding her for a reason. They had just met just a few days earlier, and she was already picturing them in bed. In her mind, she could see him ravaging her. She could almost feel his touch on her skin and smell the sweat on his. She longed for that moment but feared that it would never happen.

After having another lonely dinner where she was surrounded by happy couples, she decided to check out the steam room. She was extremely nervous. After checking to make sure it was empty she slipped on a towel and headed inside.

It was her first time in a steam room, and she found it to be quite relaxing. She leaned back and closed her eyes. She was so relaxed that she never heard the door open. Never heard someone approaching her. Suddenly she felt a finger brush a curl from her forehead.

Her eyes flew open, and she immediately sat up. Standing in front of her was Demetri, and he was wearing nothing but a towel. The sweat glistened on his muscular body. His hair was slicked back, and the beads of sweat were running down his face. For a few brief seconds, she was frozen in place. Her body was yearning for his touch.

She watched as he extended his hand to her and gently placed her hand in his. He helped her to her feet and pulled her close. She stared into his deep blue eyes as he playfully ran his finger down her face and touched her moist lips that were already starting to part. She reached out and touched his chest. Running her thumb down across his nipple. Her heart began to pound as he drew her closer. Demetri leaned in and kissed her softly on the lips. Electricity ran through her veins as he playfully toyed with her lips. He then reached down and unfastened her towel. She could feel it drop to the floor and her sudden nakedness made her shyly try to cover to her body.

Demetri reached down and peeled her hands off her sweaty body and placed them on his chest. He then unfastened his towel and drew her near. She could feel his nakedness, and it made her quiver. She opened her mouth as he leaned in and kissed her.

The passion she felt at that moment was so intense that she didn't want it to end. She wanted him to make love to her, but instead, he pulled away. He gave her a smile and told her to be patient.

"I want things to be just right," he said, kissing her lips just once more.

She watched as he put his towel back on and walked out of the door. She was sweating and shaking at the same time. Grabbing her towel, she fastened it and walked out. When she had made it back to her room, she found an invitation waiting for her. It was from Demetri who was asking her to join him for dinner that night.

Excitedly, she ran to her suitcases and tried to find something decent to wear. However, she found she had nothing that would do. She wanted something sexy. Something that would make Demetri unable to control himself.

Haven quickly took a trip into town where she purchased a sexy black dress with a low neckline that revealed her cleavage. It seemed as though the hours were just flying by as she got ready that afternoon.

When she made it to dinner, Haven found that there was no Demetri. Fearing that she had been stood up, she tried to hide her disappointment to those in the room. Not wanting the evening to go to waste, she found a seat by the window and sat down. As the happy couples around her laughed and kissed, she was on the verge of tears until someone placed a hand on her shoulder. She turned to find Demetri standing behind her.

He looked dashingly handsome wearing a deep purple dress shirt and black trousers. Just the mere sight of him took her breath away. As he sat down across from her, she could feel the electricity flowing through her veins.

For the first time in years, she was on a date, but this time she was sitting across from a man she felt a real connection with. They laughed and talked for what seemed like hours. As the champagne flowed, she began to loosen up even more. When dinner had ended, he escorted her back to her room.

Before she could open the door, he pulled her close to him and kissed her. As their tounges intertwined, she could feel him gently pressing her against the door. She wrapped her arms around him and didn't let go. She could feel him fumbling with the doorknob and heard it unclick. Soon they were entering her room and into the darkness.

In the moonlight coming from the window, she could see his smiling face. He unzipped the back of her dress and watched as it dropped to her feet. She reached out and began unbuttoning his shirt. When she had peeled it away, Haven began running her hands down his chest. He pulled her close and held her pressed tightly against his body. She could feel his hardness as she squirmed against his hips. Quickly removing his shirt, she began unfastening his belt. He led her over to the bed as he finished undressing.

Once naked, he crawled on top of her as she wrapped her legs around his hips. She needed him. Needed to feel him inside of her. Needed to taste his lips upon hers. For a while, he seemed to toy with her. He knew she was ready but wanted her to be patient.

"Patience my love," he whispered in her ear.

Just feeling his breath on her neck made her body slowly shake. As he began to explore her body, she couldn't help but feel a bit self-conscious. She wasn't exactly in shape, and there were flabby areas she couldn't hide. But just as she was about to hide her belly he gently moved her hand away. He raised her hand to his lips and kissed it softly. Haven felt him entering her body, and it was at that moment that she felt her body shake with pleasure.

She wrapped her legs around his hips and pulled him closer as she touched his lips with the tip of her tongue. His body was rock hard, and she could feel the heat radiating from him. As the passion exploded between them, she could feel her body rising. It was as though she were on a roller coaster and it was a ride she didn't want to end.

Finally, with their bodies glistening with sweat, they fell into each other's arms. He held her close to him and gently kissed her forehead. As she ran her hand down his chest, he let out a sigh. Blissfully they fell asleep.

In the morning, she awoke with her new lover kissing and biting her shoulder.

"Ready for more," he whispered. As he traced his fingers down her arm, she felt her body tremble.

"Of course," she said as she turned to face him. "I'm always ready."

He pulled her close and nuzzled her neck as she ran her fingers down his spine. That morning it was pure bliss. Her body craved him. His kisses left her weak in the knees, and she loved it.

After they had finished their lovemaking, they enjoyed a light lunch then walked along the edge of the cliff. They held hands and watched as the waves crashed against the rocks. Each morning they worked out together before class. She felt at ease with Demetri, and everything just felt right. She had never been happier in her life.

However, her happiness would soon hit a roadblock when Demetri's visits became less and less. She began to wonder if she made the right decision in sleeping with him. Perhaps that was all he was interested in. Then she spotted him talking with Jennifer.

Though she convinced herself that they were just talking, she couldn't help but feel threatened. *Am I losing the man that I'm falling in love with?* Part of her wanted to confront him, but instead, she walked away.

Choking back tears she walked the grounds of the resort for almost an hour. It wasn't until she made it back to her room that she finally sobbed. Though her reservations were still good for another week, she decided that perhaps she should leave now. There was nothing keeping her there and the longer she went without seeing Demetri, the worse she felt.

Despite the pain that she felt, she decided to leave him a letter. She explained that she was leaving and that she had no regrets. The time they spent together she would always remember. Lastly, she wished he and Jennifer the best. Slipping it under his door, she turned and walked away. Grabbing her bags, she checked out and headed towards her car. As she headed out of the parking lot, she couldn't help but wish that he would have stopped her.

Just as she was heading into town, someone on a motorcycle came up behind her. When they hit the red light, the stranger came up beside her and took off his helmet. It was Demetri, and he was motioning for her to pull over.

As she pulled off the road, she tried to stay calm. She didn't want him to see her cry. He came up beside her and opened the door.

"Haven, what are you doing?" he asked.

"I'm leaving, I'm going back home," she said as she wiped the tears from her eyes.

He reached out and wiped the tears. "I'm sorry if I seemed distant. It's just that we were getting so close and I was trying to figure out how to handle this."

She leaned against the car and stared into his deep blue eyes. "What is there to figure out? You either want to be with me, or you don't."

He gave her a smile and stroked her cheek. "Haven you are quite a woman. I have never met anyone like you. You make me feel alive," he said.

"What about Jennifer? I saw you two together," she sobbed.

"She is my co-worker and nothing else. It's you I want to be with. It's you that I want to build a future with," he said.

She looked into his eyes and stroked his cheek. He wanted to be with her, and she couldn't deny that she wanted to be with him. "So what to we do now? How do we begin this life together?" she asked pulling him closer to her.

"We take it one day at a time," he said putting his arm around her waist. Demetri pulled her close and kiss her passionately.

It was at that moment that she knew what 'happily ever after' really felt like. After years of never knowing what love was she had finally found it, and it was something she would never let go.

The Disciple

Stuart Stromin

Pandora came in at the last minute, as a replacement for one of the other performers. The first time they met was in her dressing room, and Roark spent a half hour getting to know her, which was far too long when he was needed on the set, and the assistant director had to come looking for him. She photographed well, and exuded a magnetic presence on screen, and she was so easy to work with that he did not understand why she had a reputation for being difficult, in fact, psychotic.

He should have seen the clues in her eyes, which were hazel and limpid, but which flashed with a fiery glow that he had only ever seen once before in a cinematographer who was ultimately committed to an asylum. She was tall with straight, dirty blonde hair and a sinewy tanned body, with apple-sized breasts and a famous round rump.

After the movie had wrapped, he did not give her another thought until he ran into her months later at the Cannes Film Festival in the south of France. They were at a press dinner, and he went over to her table, picking up the conversation where they had left off in the dressing room on the North Hollywood sound stage when she was doing his movie.

She was dressed in a shimmering evening gown, and he was in a tuxedo. They sat at a round ten-person table with an elaborate floral centerpiece and white tablecloth, flecked with breadcrumbs. He was planning to shoot something else in Cannes—he had brought a star in tow with him from Los Angeles—but he thought that there might be a role in it for Pandora too.

He was staying at a villa in the hills with the French producer named Philippe, among a group of international houseguests who were there for the festival or the production. Roark was the only one of the Americans who could speak French, and Philippe was the only Frenchman who could speak English, and so, with no other common languages, the two of them had to translate for everyone else in the group.

Pandora came to stay there after a few days, while they were making the movie, but they all had their own rooms, and the star who had come with him from Los Angeles did not like the way that Pandora behaved around him, making eyes, and sharing private jokes. They sat side-by-side at every meal, and sometimes picked the hors d'oeuvres off one another's plate.

The production and the festival came to an end, and everyone who was staying in the house began peeling off one by one to different destinations. Some returned to L.A., some journeyed on to other European locations.

One morning, when Philippe was shuttling the last of the guests along the coastal freeway to the airport in Nice, Roark and Pandora were left alone in the villa for the first time.

He locked the front door from the inside so that they would not be accidentally disturbed. He could not find her.

He checked her room—the door was wide open—then he went downstairs, out to the swimming pool, but she was not anywhere to be found, almost as if she were hiding. He called out for her, but she did not respond, like they were playing some sort of cat-and-mouse game. He went back into the house, and from the far end of the hallway, he saw her coming out of a spare bedroom, barefoot on the hardwood floors, wearing nothing but cut-off shorts and a pink tank top. She caught sight of him, and there was a flicker of fear in her eyes, and she darted back into her own room, and tried to close the door.

In a few strides, he ran down the corridor before she could get the door shut, he pushed it open, and she was right in front of him, afraid to move. Before they knew what they were doing, he slapped her across the face. The sting of his palm was like an electric shock.

"We're finally alone," he taunted, "There's nobody in the house to save you."

All of their flirting and innuendoes had led up to this. She fell back onto the bed, and he got on top of her. He groped her and fondled her, holding her down by clutching a handful of her hair. She fought back. She tried to kick him and knee him in the groin, so he smothered her with his weight and strength. She bit into his shoulder—so hard that there were teeth marks—and he got his forearm across her mouth. She tried to scratch him with her long polished fingernails, so he grabbed hold of her wrists and pinned her like a child having a tantrum until she stopped struggling. They lay like that face to face, fully clothed, breathing heavily, grinding together, feeling the heat of one another's bodies.

Then they heard the front door open, Philippe was back from the airport, with his keys in his hand.

"Why is everything locked?" Philippe asked.

They came out of her room, and Philippe could tell that he had interrupted something, like the witness to a crime in progress. They all went out to the pool and lay on the chaises-longues. Speaking in French, Philippe reminded Roark about his wife in Los Angeles.

Pandora caught the gist of it, and asked, "So you're married?"

"Yes." Roark looked into her glimmering eyes. "I want to be clear about that."

"I am supposed to go to Italy tomorrow," she said.

"I am going to Paris," he told her, "Why don't you come to Paris with me?"

Before she even had a chance to respond, Philippe said, "If you have never been to Paris, you have to go to Paris."

On their last night in Cannes, they slept in separate rooms, on different floors of the villa, but, as he lay in bed, Roark thought about what he had done to her in the afternoon and what he was going to do to her when they got to Paris the next day. It was all about to unfold.

Philippe drove them to the airport in Nice, and they said their good-byes. Roark and Pandora checked in for the flight, and as they went towards the gate, he reached down, and for the first time, they linked hands, twisting their fingers together.

In Paris, they stayed at a three-star hotel in Montparnasse, above a bistro and a bakery. They were on the second floor up a spiral staircase. The room was spacious by Parisian standards, at an odd L-shape, dark with faded lime wallpaper and heavy furniture under a musty smell. There was an armoire on ball-and-claw legs, a bulky chest of drawers made of dark wood, and a solid bed with a soft mattress. Through the lace curtains of the French windows, standing at the black, metal grillwork, they could see down to the terrace of the bistro, decked with umbrellas branded with the advertising logos of popular aperitifs, and beyond, across the gray roofs and chimney pots of Paris.

That night, he stripped her naked and posed her on all fours on top of the chest of drawers. Her long hair hung down, her eyes were blindfolded with her own scarf. She moaned and whimpered as he teased her for hours, exploring every pore of her body.

Pandora did not travel without her own crop, and he used it on her gently at first, but she wanted it harder and harder. He never had the sang-froid to crop her as hard as she desired, no matter how she begged for it. It was not enough for her if there weren't welts and bruises painted across her buttocks. She wanted to be marked, for the pure adrenaline rush of it, and so that she could savor the experience afterward, and maintain a sense of submission to him.

In the morning, with the sun streaming across the Parisian rooftops, they lay in bed together as if they had known one another since they were teenage sweethearts. The smell of freshly-baked baguettes rose from the bakery. The lace curtains fluttered in the window-frame. Together in their room, it seemed like there was nobody else in the entire world, as if the planet had ceased turning on its axis, and come to a sudden halt.

They rode the Metro from Montparnasse rattling along the grimy underground tunnels to the opulence of the Champs-Elysees, and before they came up the escalator from the station to the street, he covered her eyes with his hands. He led her out to the traffic island in the center of the grand Avenue, in the midst of all the squeaky horns and clatter, and pointed her so that when he took his hands away, she was staring up at the Arc de Triomphe.

"Now, whenever you see a picture of this monument, in a movie or a magazine, you will always think of me," he said.

As the sun fell, they had a leisurely dinner at a quiet restaurant on the left bank. They sat outside in the languor of the evening, and ate oysters and torteau on a bed of crushed ice, with a bottle of Muscadet. A boy came by with a basket of roses for sale, and he bought Pandora a single stem. After dinner, they strolled along the Seine, past the looming gothic cathedral of Notre-Dame, and watched the bateaux-mouches chugging down the river and beneath the old bridges. Lights from the boats and from the banks reflected on the ripples. Under the streetlamps, with a spring breeze drifting through her hair, she looked so young and beautiful that he could not believe that she was on his arm.

"I hope she costs you a fortune," a passer-by yelled at him in French.

Roark translated for Pandora, and they all laughed about it.

On the way back to where they were staying, they found themselves alone on a cobblestone street. He ordered her to get on her knees on the dirty stones, and kiss his boots.

Instantly acquiescent, she dropped, leaving an imprint of her fresh red lipstick pressed in supplication against the leather toe of his boot, like the crimson rose resting on the sullen ground. He cupped the heel of his other boot on the back of her neck, keeping her in place. They did not move from the provocative tableau, understanding that the longer they remained in position, the more risk there would be of being discovered. Nobody came, and he gently raised her to his lips, and they kissed—closed mouthed—like a father and child, rather than lovers.

Back in the little world of their little room, he tied her wrists to the metal grillwork at the window with one of his silk ties, and leaned her over the railing with her breasts exposed, and her famous bottom towards him. He slipped off his belt, and with one stroke after another, he left a row of warm stripes on her flesh. She cried out in ecstasy with every crack, and from the terrace of the bistro downstairs, two men sipping *digestifs* looked up, and watched, grinning.

"Everybody can see what you are," he told her, holding the back of her skull so that she could not avoid their brazen stare.

They raised their glasses to toast her, one of them whistled.

She felt so ashamed and exposed that her face flushed. She was sure that the men on the terrace could hear the slap of the belt each time he struck her. The breeze rose again, billowing the lace curtains, and the coolness of the air touched the heat of her flesh where his leather strap was marking her scarlet.

"More," she gasped, "Harder. I need it hard. Please."

"No," he said, coiling up the belt, "You've had enough. I will beat you again tomorrow. Now, say thank you like a good little girl."

"Thank you, sir."

The thorny rose stood in a glass of water on the chest of drawers. He put the cool glass against her marks and caressed her with a soothing touch. Nimbly, he untied the silken knots, rubbed her wrists, and helped her upright. She swooned in his strong arms. He laid her on her back on top of the bed sheets, with her soft long hair on the white pillow. He unbuttoned his shirt and dropped out of his beltless slacks. Roark lay down beside her, resting on his hip and elbow, and looked down into her eyes.

She gazed dreamily at him. "You swear you've never done this before?"

"Done what?"

"You know." Pandora gave a coy smile, and her voice got husky. "Played this game."

"Not like you have."

"You are better at it than the Master I had before, and he had done it for years."

"Well," he said, with that playful arrogance that aroused her all over again, "We're just getting started."

The second year that they were in Cannes together, they shared a suite at a luxurious resort hotel overlooking the gulf. There were colorful tiles on the floor, and soft watercolor paintings on the walls, and because they were on a high floor, they could leave the balcony doors open all day for the fresh sea air. Yachts and motorboats sailed across the water; vacationers sunbathed topless on the narrow private beach. The executives and filmmakers who were there for the market did business in short pants and short sleeves.

Everyone knew that they were a couple, but the journalists covering the Festival kept their names out of the papers because they all understood that he was married.

That was not easy to juggle in L.A., and to her credit, because he had a wife, she had resisted when he first tried to follow up the affair in their hometown. But they were drawn to each other as if it was destiny, and there was no way to contain their passion.

They met at hotel rooms in the short afternoons; sometimes, they spotted another pair of cheats in the hotel bar, giggling over a cozy cocktail, before making their way upstairs. They snuck away on weekends. They went down the coast, or up into the mountains to his cabin when there was snow.

On special occasions, he rented a dungeon from a downtown bondage parlor, which offered hourly rates in black-walled rooms with mirrors, cages, hoists, beams, slings and coffins. Some of the women who worked there were always lounging around in frilly undergarments in the front lobby, where they paid for the rental, and they all looked Roark and Pandora up and down, knowing that he was her Master and she was his slave. She could not raise her eyes to meet their gaze while she was wearing the collar.

They spoke on the telephone three or four times a day; first thing to say good morning, and always last thing late at night, murmuring fantasies. And there was always something to arrange, to plan, to share, and any other excuse to talk to one another through the long illicit day.

Roark cast her in all his projects, sometimes as the lead, sometimes in a supporting role. Their careers blossomed together, and because of her reputation, he was considered one of the few directors who knew how to handle her.

On the set, they squabbled sometimes, but it was mostly a kind of foreplay, because they knew that after work, they would play. There was always that undercurrent running through everything they did, and none of it was any secret from the crew. Sometimes, they would slip into a nook somewhere on the location, and he would manhandle her, in a stolen moment, with his hand up her skirt, and whispering filthy threats in her ear, and they would emerge and separate, as if nothing had happened, but nobody was fooled.

All of the sneaking around added intrigue and excitement to their affair, but they could not help wanting it to be somehow out in the open. They could not wait to return to Cannes, as the year rolled by and the festival came closer.

In Cannes, their romance was evident to everyone in the hotel, from the guests to the waiters, and because there was such closeness and passion between them, and she was so extraordinarily radiant, they charmed and dazzled.

There was a bartender at the downstairs bar, Jean-Marc, who became his confidant, and when the bar was jammed, like it was most nights, Roark could always get a drink quickly. He spent most of the days in chaotic meetings with distributors, financiers, and producers, all over the Croisette, while Pandora did the press junket, with the paparazzi. They were both under pressure, although they relished the whir of activity; him, in his deals and visions, her in the flash of the cameras.

By the time evening fell, they craved each other. In the night, they were inseparable. They met back in the room, and whoever got there first laid out the gear. As soon as they saw each other, they played. They played before they went out, and they raced home to play before they succumbed to sleep. They let off steam. They got close. There was a casino in the resort, and she always liked to gamble. There were cocktails and dinners and parties and soirees, and hardly any time left in the small hours to sleep, before it all began again the next morning with breakfast meetings.

He did not have a movie to make that year, but since they were there together, he decided to shoot some footage of her that they might be able to incorporate into a future project. He liked directing her, and she adored being on camera. He filmed her walking in the streets on a shopping expedition, with her arms full of packages, and riding the carousel along the beachfront. She was wearing a white dress with the sunlight hitting her at an angle from behind to give her rim lighting, and her blonde hair like golden straw. He set up a shot of her crossing the old stone square from the church to the fountain, during which he told her to look sad. He did not know what use the footage would be, but she would look beautiful when he added a voiceover and music.

After the festival, they flew to Paris again and stayed in their same hotel above the bakery in Montparnasse. Philippe was in the capital on business with the banks, and they all went to lunch together at the Drugstore on the Champs-Elysees.

They ate salad with goat cheese, and steak au poivre with frites, and went through two bottles of Beaujolais among the three of them.

Philippe said in French, "You are not continental, Roark. You speak the language, but you are an American. She is beautiful, but you are never going to get away with this."

"I have things under control," he replied in French.

"Speak English," Pandora complained, with a girly whine.

"You be quiet, little girl," he ordered her, because he knew she was acting up for Philippe's benefit.

"Yes, sir," she said, coyly lowering her eyes.

"I see what you mean," Philippe said, in French, "So, you will never accept my advice. You are both in love. But you are going to get hurt in the end. Everyone does."

Philippe, to show his understanding, told them about a fetish club near Pigalle. He had no interest in that sort of thing, but he had all sorts of friends, and he knew Paris well.

It was a French Normandy-style building with decorative turrets, in the shadow of the hill of Montmartre with the white dome of the Sacre-Coeur church swelling above it. There were not many people there when Roark and Pandora arrived, and it seemed much larger from outside. It was dimly lit, and there was a bar and a lounge with a small dance floor. Down a short flight of stairs, there was a wood-paneled basement with a padded black bench and a wooden bondage cross, and sconces for candles on the wall. A strange Frenchman in a leather hood held her down while Roark penetrated her. She looked so frightened and uncomfortable; she was afraid that he was going to offer her to the other man, but he was just keeping her on the edge.

"Beat me," she begged, "I need a beating."

"I will decide when you require punishment."

"Please!" There were tears in her wild eyes. "I am begging you, please."

She hungered for pain; she was so deep in her subspace that she felt numb. He buckled her wrists into padded cuffs with spring-loaded catches so that he could hook her hands to the cross, with her bare back towards him. There was somber music playing, and she arched and swayed, held by the wristlets. The Frenchman in the hood offered him a whip.

Roark flicked the whip and, in a series of criss-cross motions, marked a pattern of red lines across her back.

Pandora threw her head back, with a whimper each time the leather coils touched her.

He lowered the whip, and pressed his body against her, soothing the marks with his fingers. He grabbed a handful of hair and pulled her head back towards him.

"That's enough for you," he whispered, with his mouth against her ear.

"No," she gulped, shaking her head, "Please, more. Harder. I need it hard."

He struck her again, and the whip bit into her flesh like a thunderclap.

"More!" she gasped, and then through her teeth, one word at a time, she said, "Is that all you got?"

With a strong arm, the angry lash came crashing down. Roark could not help wincing when he saw the instant welts forming on her flesh.

There was a hand on his shoulder, and it was the bouncer from the club.

"You both have to leave," the bouncer instructed.

"She likes it," Roark explained, "She wants it."

Pandora twisted around. "I am okay."

"You have to leave."

It was a warm evening on the street outside, but Pandora was trembling from all the emotion of the beating. He gently put his arms around her.

She giggled. "I can't believe that we got thrown out of a fetish club for being too rough."

"They have never seen anything like us before," he said, waving down a taxi so that they could continue what they had started back at the hotel.

On the day before they were to return to America, they ascended the Eiffel tower together, taking the third elevator right to the very top. It was the most romantic moment of her life, and she told him that she loved him.

As the sun fell, the sweeping panorama of Paris sprawled beneath them, with its famous palaces and parks, and the undulating Seine, and the hulking silhouettes of Notre-Dame and the Arc de Triomphe. The golden sunlight glistened on the river as the dark shadows of the monuments stretched longer in the gloaming.

Roark and Pandora were as high as clouds on the lofty platform. She could not stare down for too long because it made her dizzy.

He drew her close with one hand on the nape of her neck, and the other hand firmly cupped between her thighs.

"Why are you so wet?" he teased.

"For you," Pandora confessed, "For you, sir. You make me wet."

"Who owns you?"

The lights of the city twinkled all the way to the horizon.

"You do, sir," she breathed, gazing limpidly into his eyes, "You will be my Master forever."

She rented a house on the beach in Malibu, because it was cheap through the winter. It was a poky, windswept place, not in the best repair, made of planks hammered together, but it was right on the sand. That first afternoon, they rolled up their jeans and went barefoot down to the water. There were wooden pilings under a structure, and she dragged him into the shadows split by the lines of sunlight glinting through the splintery boards above. They made love in the sand, in broad daylight, but there was nobody to disturb them, except the white caplets of the cobalt waves.

There was a large deck upstairs, and at night, she put stout candles on the railings which burned down quickly because of the sea air. They stood in the candlelight, sipping white wine from oversized glasses, and looked out at the unruly surf. She was a siren in the glow of the candles, standing at the railing against the luminous sea. The breakers rolled in one by one, the silence of the beach was broken only by the fizzy hiss of the ocean. She kept waiting for him to say that he was going to leave his wife, but he never said it. It was on the tip of his tongue, but he never said it.

He did not leave his wife—not then, not for her—and Pandora did not want to wait any longer. There were other suitors; it was not fair. There were random men who were interested. He was always jealous of them, the way that she was jealous of his marriage. There was something to quarrel about almost every day. A cheat himself, he wondered if she were cheating on him. The whole affair had left them both exhausted. He knew it was going to be over soon, but he loved her still.

Things started to get ugly; Pandora left deliberate clues, his wife suspected. There was tension at home. Pandora made her own dalliances obvious. He had never been on the receiving end of it, but now he began to understand why the actress had such a reputation for being temperamental.

That year, the third year in Cannes, they stayed in separate suites, but they were in the same resort hotel on the bay. They went out for dinner to the Italian pizzeria across from the marina, which was open late at night, and served runny pizzas in the European style straight from the oven. They drank a few beers, and it felt like old times, but they did not play together.

They attended some of the same events, during the festival, but they were both always busy in conversations and only waved and smiled across the room. They saw each other at the bar of the hotel, but they did not go up to each other's suites, even though he kept trying to entice her.

Jean-Marc was no longer at the bar downstairs; he had left to open up his own café further down the coast in Saint Tropez. Roark missed his camaraderie. The new bartender was thin, pale and obsequious. The ambiance was not the same. The hotel had completed a renovation. The layout of the room had changed, drapes spoiled the sea view. All the old ways of being charming did not work anymore.

"Why don't you come back to Paris again with me?" he asked her.

"I am here with two other girls," she told him, "We are all leaving together."

She did not say goodbye when the time came to depart.

He came down on the morning she was supposed to leave, just in time to watch the luxury coach to the airport rumbling down the hotel driveway.

"Did the girls leave?" he asked the hotel porter in French.

He pointed to the bus with a white glove. "There they go."

"In tears?"

"No." The porter shook his head because he understood why Roark had asked the question. "They were happy."

He went to Paris on his own, with an empty seat beside him on the airplane, and walked for miles along the lonely streets. He was in no rush to return home, to the wreckage of his marriage, and he stayed in Paris in an apartment hotel on the right bank near Les Halles for longer than he had planned.

As luck would have it, her photograph was on that month's cover of one of the French celebrity magazines. Wherever he went, she stared at him from the newsstands, and along the boulevards, there were billboards with her face. It was a bitter torment. The gods were having fun at his expense. He wandered the sidewalks alone, past all their old haunts, and there was no way not to think about her.

He thought about all those nights in secret rooms; the whisk of a flogger, the chomp of handcuffs, the frightened look in her wild eyes, the whimper of surrender, the private intimacies, the quiet bond of trust and understanding. He watched the old footage, when she was so young and beautiful, but he did not feel melancholy. It was cold fire. It was history, and there were monumental marks left in his psyche like landmarks to show him the way.

They met one final time at a bar on Ventura Boulevard when they were back in California. After they had a drink, while they were waiting for the valet, they hugged goodbye, and then Roark watched her red taillights disappearing down the long boulevard. He was tired from chasing her for all those years, and he knew he would not pursue her anymore. He let her go.

He thought about what she had done for him, and what she had taught him. She had transformed him. Like it often is when a woman leaves you, he would never be the same man again.

He was keen to explore the future, and he understood that she would fade into the past. She was a good memory, he was proud that she had worn his collar for a time. He considered that, somehow or another, we are all teachers and all students, here to expose knowledge to one another. He would never forget her. He would always be grateful for what he had learned as her one-time Master, as her Master forever, and as her ultimate disciple.

The Flowers Always Die

Bretton B. Holmes

She is outside at present, somewhere in the backyard. I can't see her at the moment because I am inside and I have the shades drawn.

Call it my superstition. I've never been able to write when the sun comes through a window. She always asks me why I don't write outside in the gazebo and I just shrug. I suppose it has to do with the sun and the fact that I wasn't the one who built the thing. The gazebo, not the sun. But every so often I move from my haven here at the desk to stroll into the kitchen, where there comes a burst of light through the banana yellow lace curtains above the sink.

I find that I most often head in there when my drink is down. I walk across the padded carpet, some shade of brown I don't know the name of and find myself reaching for a paper towel to refresh the glass from its condensation. I don't allow myself to look until I have my next drink ready. There's something definitive about the anticipation of being ready, of having the drink in my hand, listening to the cubes clink welcomingly as I stand before the sink, eyes closed with the first sip and then, open to the expanse of the backyard.

I sometimes will not see her at first, and there is a slight panic I feel that she has gone somewhere, even though I know that she is out there somewhere. I scan the grounds there and see a knee poking out from the corner of the window above the sink. I move slightly, and her form is revealed, almost like opening a present.

The sight of her there crouched in front of a neat row of azaleas brings me to pause, standing there as I do, the faint smell of some good meal we'd eaten the night before filling my nostrils. It's not because I haven't done the dishes mind you; the smell is more of the lingering variety. The way the brain remembers where you were when the meal transpired, and if you concentrate hard enough, you remember. The 'tones' I've heard a friend say.

Dinners around here with the two of us are something of an event. We try things we don't try normally. Sometimes we get it right; so right that the meals border on the epic, and sometimes they are just meals, but they are always eaten with great relish, and the anticipation of the next to come is heightened. And there she is, a flower among the flowers.

Time stands still in these moments for me. I drink my drink as I drink in the view. I see the curves of her, beautiful in their simplicity. I have seen how other men look at her when we do the shopping when the week starts, and it's as if they were thinking of something and then, upon seeing her, are at a complete loss as to what it might have been. I suspect it is the way she walks. She walks from her center, with her feet pointed out at slight angles, not so much like one might imagine a duck, more, it elicits thoughts of high-heeled feet in the air, head thrown back, the tongue licks the lips in some undulation of ecstasy, the slight angles of the feet give suggestion to what lurks further up. Just the thought of having seen her in that way makes me long for the next time. I have studied how she walks both coming and going, and that, coupled with a long slim neck accentuated by hair that falls just above the shoulder, well, she walks as though she invented sex.

I exhale there forcefully in front of the sink, getting a bit light-headed from the drink in my hand and the sight of her in shorts, sandals and tube top that accentuates the curve of her breasts. There is the hat too, which she once wore in the shed during an impromptu break I'd taken from writing. Sandals and a hat and it will stay with me forever I am sure.

It is difficult to go back into the office in these moments, but the typer beckons. I entertain anxious thoughts of how it was that I found myself here in the first place.

***

We met at the memorial service of her sixteen-year-old son. I'd been heading down the pier toward where my Swan 50 was docked, the only thing I'd been awarded in my divorce some years prior. I still live there. It's fine, I don't need much space to write. The desk in the office here is like writing on an expanse compared to the navigational area of the boat.

A throng of people were down by the slip, about forty or fifty feet from the boat. Unusual since it wasn't a holiday or a weekend. A Tuesday in fact, if I recall correctly. At any rate, it was strange, and I immediately took it to be someone who'd purchased a new boat and was about the christen it some awfully unseaworthy name. I didn't pay it much mind until I saw the urn come out.

That was when I first saw her, bending down at the pier's edge. She was wearing a skirt, strappy heels, and a sleeveless white button-down shirt. I've always had a thing for good lines, and she had good lines. She was crying as she knelt there with the urn holding her son who'd gone long before he should have. As I understand it, he was in a car with some members of his high school tennis team and they came around a blind curve and a driver hit them. The driver wasn't drunk, it was some other substance.

I watched from the window of my boat as the memorial service came to a close and everyone began paying their respects. She didn't stand up, she just stayed there, sobbing over the water, the tears mixing with the ash floating there. A tall man stood over her looking out across the water. I assumed that it was the priest or reverend or whatever they call them now. After a few minutes, he looked down at her there as she was sobbing. He said something then walked back up the pier. She stayed there awhile without moving, and I suddenly had the idea that something might be wrong. I've heard of people going catatonic at funerals, so I thought I ought to at least go topside and take a closer look to make sure she was okay. She was after all, close to the water.

I went up on the deck and peered at her then I looked up to where people usually park their cars. I went to pick up a bucket or something there so I'd look like I wasn't staring, and I see her look to where the cars were. I looked too. The man from before stood with his back up against the driver's side door of a Land Rover, arms crossed, looking back down to where she was. I saw her wave him off as if telling him to leave. He looked down, kicked the ground slightly, got in the car and left. A few moments went by, and she stood up.

I remember how I was immediately struck by her beauty, a dangerous thing for me because that was how I saw my ex-wife. Now it's just horns and a tail. But there was something almost majestic about the way she stood there on the pier, almost as if she had completed a formidable task, which of course, she had. She turned and started walking up the pier. I busied myself with something or other on the boat, thinking I'd look up as she walked past, but then she didn't, and she caught me as I looked up with her standing at the bow of my boat.

"Nice boat," she said.

"Thank you," I said. She was there in front of me, and I wasn't sure what to say next.

"Would you mind if I asked for a quick tour?"

"Not at all …"

I wasn't used to such an instant disregard for the convention of 'Hi, What's Your Name?' and 'What Do You Do?' muckety-muck. Everyone says it, but nobody really cares. We all want to skip to the jump. Questions arise in the mind like how does this person in front of me fit into my life in this moment or the next? Ridiculous when you think about it really. It's almost as if we are trying to predict the future silently.

I helped her onto the boat after advising her to take her heels off. She has beautiful toes. Ankles that are in direct proportion to the calves. Like I said, I've always appreciated good lines. She had them. As I watched her come aboard, her skirt slightly riding up the thigh, it finally made sense why men always refer to their ships as 'she.' I also became aware of the connection of women being referred to as 'built.'

"You sail this all by yourself?"

"Yes."

"It must be difficult, no? It's big."

"Well, I don't take it out much. I live on it."

"Oh. I would think it would be nice living on a boat like this. The water rocking you to sleep."

"Well, it does sometimes and then sometimes I find I can't sleep because some group of teenagers decides to take their parent's boat out."

"Can I see the inside?"

"Sure, just don't mind the mess. I don't get a lot of company."

I handed her back her shoes which she promptly proceeded to put back on. Call it sympathy for why I let her come aboard. I'm particular about the boat and who gets on it since it is the only thing I own now. 'Post-marital amenities' I say.

I have this friend, Chuck, who always laughs and says it sounds like a sexual innuendo and then I shoot back, "Yeah, it's true I got royally fucked on the deal."

"Was that a family member?" I asked.

"Huh?"

She was sort of languishing through the main cabin as I walked behind her. Great lines. I hadn't seen hips with legs like that in a long time. She moved well, good coordination. She had a beautiful frame, and she knew it. Then I remembered the urn and immediately felt guilty for being attracted to her and then a moment later thinking myself ridiculous either way.

Beautiful women didn't typically frequent the confines of my writing area unless they were in some story I happened to be working on. I didn't think the guys at the driving range would believe me, but maybe I wouldn't tell them. The thought that she might be uncomfortable being on a complete stranger's boat occurred to me, and I suddenly got very self-conscious about my manners and blurted out, "Would you like a drink?"

Before I could apologize, the answer came back, "Yes." A stout yes, as though she'd been waiting for the offer since coming aboard. I pulled two rocks glasses, reached across to the fridge for cubes and dropped them in. I've always loved that clink. Some rocks glasses don't have that clink.

She spoke, "I love that sound …"

"Huh?"

"That clink of the ice when it hits the bottom of the glass."

"Macallan okay?"

"Definitely. It was my son."

"Huh?"

"My son. You asked about the memorial."

"Oh, right. I'm … sorry."

"Well, yes, I appreciate that."

"I've always been awful at those comments. It sounds so cliché, but you can't really avoid saying it. You know, people think you're not right in the head if you don't say it."

"Is that why you said it?

"Oh, no, I mean, I don't typically say things I don't mean."

She laughed offhandedly, and I poured the Macallan into the glasses, resisting the urge to make the ice clink in its dampened state by raising it up and shaking it as if to say 'here it comes' without actually saying the thing. I saw that done in a movie once and it was complete idiocy. Things were comfortable, and I was just happy to have some company for a change. I lifted her glass to take it to her, but when I turned her hand was there around mine, and she delicately took it from me.

"Thank you," she said. She walked back over to where the table was across from the little navigational nook and sat down, crossed her legs. I took a good long haul off mine, forcing my eyes away from her legs. She smelled the whiskey like it was some kind of rare flower and I took another gulp.

"So …" she said. "You live here all alone?"

"Yes. That was your husband, on the pier?"

"Yes."

"He didn't seem—"

"Like he cared? He does as much as he can I suppose. I don't know. Seth's passing has been difficult for him, but he has that stupid macho male idea that he isn't supposed to cry. He just doesn't talk."

"That's too bad," I said.

I wasn't sure why I said it was too bad. I felt her even as she sat there with my rocks glass in her hand. My mind went to all the places that were awkward as she reached a hand down to run over the inner part of her calf. The skin there was smooth, and I watched her and found myself suddenly in a trance.

"What do they call you," she asked.

She was smiling, and I was completely embarrassed. Or 'bare-assed' as my friend always jokes. There was nothing I could say in that instant and nowhere I could phone for help, so I had to just stand there and try not to think of what my face was saying.

It must have said plenty because she stopped smiling, stood up and walked over to me. She looked up at me with our faces just inches apart. Her eyes were still red from the tears, and I could smell the salt mix with her perfume and the Macallan, and then our mouths met.

I got my drink stabilized and felt her mouth with mine. Soft and supple. Smooth and wet. I could taste the salt from her tears. I was drunk with the way she felt beneath my hands. There was a fit there. She held my face in her left hand, just so and her right hand began to unfasten my belt as I moved back for clearance.

I wanted to taste her, to feel her center on my lips, to feel her shudder from my mouth there. I ran my hands over her thighs, strong and lean to the back of her skirt. It fell to the floor, and she stepped out of the ring it made there.

I took a step back to take her form in with my eyes, with her standing there in the sleeveless button down shirt, heels and a black lace thong stretched taught over her pubic bone, the slightest hint of hair there. She slipped them down, and I saw the small tuft of black hair nestled just above her labia. With a hand, she reached down and touched herself, and with the other, she pulled me toward her and put her moistened fingers into my mouth so I could taste her.

It was musky and sweet and viscous. I got my pants off and lifted her so her buttocks were on the counter and knelt down in front of her. She slowly lifted a leg up placing it over my shoulder, and I saw her sex there, glistening. Her clitoris swelled, beckoning for my mouth to lick the sweet juice of her. I languished my tongue up the inside of her thigh, and she shuddered, her hand ran over my chest and to my neck and grabbed the hair on the back of my head as I took her labia into my mouth, felt the heat from inside her run over my tongue. She gasped, head thrown back in a series of guttural moans as I sucked there, my tongue darting in the small opening.

With my hair in her hand, she moved my head back and brought her other leg up, splaying herself with her fingers as I roamed the length of her mons with my tongue, slurping at her labia gently as I felt the hot potion from inside her, creamy and thick, ooze over my mouth.

I raised up in front of her, and she reached out a french-manicured hand to stroke my length, feeling her delicate fingers run over my testicles, tight against the base of my shaft. She got down from the counter and squatted down in front of me, her eyes looking up as she took me into her mouth, and I felt her tongue lavish me. She took off her blouse, and for the first time, I realized she was not wearing a bra. Her pink nipples jutted out, full, begging for my mouth. Her breasts were perfect teardrops, a beautiful slope and swath, full and firm. She pressed a finger at the base of me and with the tip of her tongue and teeth massaged the tip.

She looked up at me. "I want this deep inside me," she said.

She stood up, and I could see a stream of her wetness along her inner thighs. I lifted her back onto the counter, and she spread her beautiful legs once again, taking me in her hand, she rubbed herself with the tip of me and moaned.

"God you feel amazing," she said. She guided me into her ever so slowly, and I felt the tightness I'd felt with my tongue. She was swollen, and as I entered her slowly, I could feel every inch of her gripping my manhood as it went deep inside her. She gasped loudly, the look on her face one of complete and utter wanton need. I put my hands underneath her firm buttocks and plunged into her, as deep as I could. With every stroke, it felt as though she would split in half, and I could feel myself slide against her pubic bone, the warm wet heated flesh around me was taught, like tightly wrapped velvet as her body fell into a violent orgasm and she lost her breath with each thrust inside her. My mouth found her breasts and I felt the nipples as hard as I was.

We knocked a bottle of wine I'd had on the counter over onto the floor from the hard motion. I entered her deeply and picked her up still inside her and felt her entire weight bear down on me, so I was deeper than before, and she thrust herself onto me, her wetness still oozing and covering me. I felt her deep inside, the small nub there fully against my tip and she let out a long, vicious grunt as she came again.

I felt the urge to come and withdrew, holding myself at my base to stave off the ejaculate. She quickly moved to where the table was and threw herself forward on it, spreading her legs so that I could enter her from behind. I saw the ripe mounds of her taught buttocks, the curvature and the muscle underneath her soft white skin as they signaled the length of thighs down to her french-manicured toes. She looked at me as she rubbed herself, standing as she was on the tips of her toes, beckoning me to enter her from behind.

I moved to her and saw the gloriousness of her tight vagina, her fingers splaying the wet labia apart and just above, her anus, pink and hairless. I ran my hands over her buttocks, and she moaned. Placing the palm of my hand on the small of her back, I gripped myself with my other hand and guided myself into her, feeling the sides of her fingers as I entered. It was tighter this way, and she gasped for air. She moved her hands to her buttocks and pulled them apart slightly, and I plunged in deeper, reaching up and sliding my hand up the side of her hips to her breast. I went deep into her, long smooth strokes so she could feel me in her depths. I felt my center begin to convulse with every thrust inside her, the heat from her vagina bringing me closer to climax. She reached under her belly and found me just before I came inside her and groaned as I convulsed and spurted uncontrollably inside her. The semen oozed from her sex, and we were both sweating as I lowered myself on top of her, feeling the tightness of her as my penis went soft and began to slip out of her.

She went to the bathroom and came back with a towel and went to the sink. I was spent and plopped down on a chair nearest where we'd just been. I watched her beautiful form as she ran warm water over the hand-towel and came over to me and kneeling there, she cleaned me off.

"That was amazing," she said.

I couldn't say a word as I was still trying to catch my breath.

"You have a beautiful penis," she said.

"Thank you," I said. Her form caught a glimmer of the sun as it went down and as she got up to rinse the towel, I hoped it would not be the last time I heard her say those words.

***

Now every year, about this time, on the anniversary of her son's death I come stay with her for a couple of weeks. The husband always leaves before I get here; she says he can't stand the house around the anniversary and so he leaves on a trip of his own design. I try to get some writing done when I'm here, while she is out gardening, but I always come back to the kitchen to watch her, to see the thighs kneeling down as she digs at the earth. We make love in the garden at night, silently, the precursor to the ravaged lovemaking we get to after dinner inside. She will come in, dirty from gardening, sweaty and I find I can't resist her as she goes to the cupboard to get a glass for a drink of water. I will move to her, and it is like that first time on the boat, all over again.

Sometimes I ask her how the flowers outside are, but she always tells me the same thing.

"The flowers always die," she will say.

And there is nothing I can do, nothing I can say that will make it otherwise.

Contributors

Alaina Symanovich

Alaina Symanovich studies creative nonfiction in the MFA program at Florida State University. Her work has appeared or is forthcoming in Sonora Review, Superstition Review, Santa Ana River Review, and other journals.

Her essay *The M Word*, first published in Fourth River, and was awarded Best of the Net in 2016.

Bretton B. Holmes

Bretton B. Holmes holds an MFA in Playwriting from the University of Southern California.

He lives somewhere in Texas.

David Rae

David lives in Scotland. He loves the history that seems to exist just below the surface of things, like deep water. He has had a chequered career and working in a sweetie factory, as a scaffolder, a ditch digger, a draftsman, an ecologist, a statistician and a policy maker.

He currently works with numbers but plays with words. He has most recently had work published in Helios Quarterly, Gnu Magazine, The Machinery, Three Drops From The Cauldron, and 50 Word Stories.

Destiny Eve Pifer is a published journalist whose work has appeared in True Confessions, Redbook, Spotlight on Recovery and Autism Parenting Magazine.

As a news reporter for her hometown newspaper, she enjoys writing human interest stories.

Kevin Breen

Kevin Breen is a short story writer from Michigan. His work has appeared in about twenty-five journals, most recently in New Orleans Review, Bayou Magazine, Natural Bridge, and Clackamas Review.

E. W. Farnsworth

E. W. Farnsworth, an Arizona writer, is widely published online and in print.

For updates, please see www.ewfarnsworth.com.

Norman Klein

Norman Klein has an Iowa MFA and has published fifteen stories in the last fifteen months—all of them in lit mags or anthologies. He read and edited for Ploughshares while teaching in Boston, then moved on to Chicago to break records for 'time spent in jazz bars.'

However, he now lives and writes in the back woods of New Hampshire.

Stuart Stromin

Stuart Stromin is a South African-born writer and filmmaker, living in Los Angeles. He was educated at Rhodes University, South Africa, the Alliance Francais de Paris, and UCLA.

He has two children, a cat, and a dog.

Vincent Salvati

Vincent Salvati was born and raised in New Jersey. He is a graduate of Pratt Institute, Montclair State University, and William Paterson University.

An author, poet, and visual artist, he strives for creativity in his work and his life. He has previously written and performed in the New York City area, and his work can be found in a variety of publications including *Typehouse Literary Magazine*, *Fabula Argentea*, and *The Paterson Literary Review*. Among his many solo and group exhibitions is his inclusion in the New Jersey Arts Annual at the Montclair Art Museum. He is currently on the board of directors for the Jersey City based non-profit, Pro Arts.

An avid traveler, he loves learning about different cultures. When he isn't creating, he can be found trekking around one continent or another. Vincent currently lives and works in New Jersey.

A Note from the Publisher

How to Thank a Contributor

Dear Reader,

Everyone at Temptation Press would like to thank you for reading *Summer Fling: Tales of Seduction.* If you would like to thank a particular contributor, the best way is to leave a review for them. You may do so by leaving one on our Goodreads page, under the *"Summer Fling"* title, and be sure to mention the contributor directly.

Why leave a review? Reviews help budding authors build their credibility in the book industry. By posting a review on Goodreads, you help other readers find new authors they may wish to follow, and you never know, your review may end up on an author's website one day.

***